"I want to feed him. Show me what to do."

Alik stood too close. Blaire could feel his warmth. The familiar brand of soap Alik used in the shower emanated from his bronzed skin, assailing Blaire's senses.

She placed a clean cloth over his broad shoulder, careful not to touch him for fear she wouldn't want to stop. Then she handed him the bottle.

"Go ahead and put it in his mouth. He'll do the rest."

When Alik did her bidding, the baby started devouring his formula. He drank so fast and furiously, he made loud noises that sounded indecent. Alik's laughter started in his throat and rumbled out to fill the hotel room.

She couldn't help smiling. "As you're discovering, he has your healthy appetite." Before she gave her feelings away, she moved to the other bed. "Do you want me to leave the light on or off?"

"On," Alik murmured. "I still have trouble believing he's real."

D1538416

Meet

Dominic, Alik and Zane

Three firm friends…
Three successful business partners…
Three dedicated bachelors…

But life is full of surprises, and these gorgeous men
are about to discover the joys of fatherhood—
and of marriage—sooner than they think!

Surprised by fatherhood and ready for love!

Next month in
The Baby Discovery by Rebecca Winters,
Zane finds an abandoned baby—
don't miss it!

HIS VERY OWN BABY
Rebecca Winters

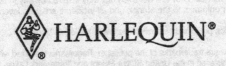

TORONTO • NEW YORK • LONDON
AMSTERDAM • PARIS • SYDNEY • HAMBURG
STOCKHOLM • ATHENS • TOKYO • MILAN • MADRID
PRAGUE • WARSAW • BUDAPEST • AUCKLAND

ISBN 0-373-03635-3

HIS VERY OWN BABY

First North American Publication 2001.

This edition published by arrangement with Harlequin Books S.A.

® and TM are trademarks of the publisher. Trademarks indicated with
® are registered in the United States Patent and Trademark Office, the
Canadian Trade Marks Office and in other countries.

Visit us at www.eHarlequin.com

Printed in U.S.A.

CHAPTER ONE

BLAIRE REGAN got out of the rental car and locked the door. She could smell rain in the early-morning air. It wouldn't be long before it started falling.

After glancing around the excavation site outside Warwick, New York, she walked over to a couple of college students emerging from one of several dozen trailers.

"Excuse me? Could you tell me where I might find Dr. Alik Jarman? I was told he's the consulting geologist on this project."

It had taken several days and many costly, long-distance phone calls to various universities to determine his exact whereabouts in this pastoral section of the state.

Both heads turned at the same time. The look of blatant male admiration was always flattering, but right now she was too frightened and nervous to appreciate their attention. Her legs were shaking so hard it was a miracle she could still stand, let alone walk.

The blond one smiled. "He's living in the trailer at the far end."

By some miracle she'd arrived at the right place.

His buddy asked, "Are you one of Dr. Fawson's students from New York University?" Hope shone brightly from a pair of warm blue eyes.

Her reason for being here was no one else's business, but she couldn't blame them for flirting. It was early October. College classes had barely started.

5

Naturally they'd assumed she'd come to join the other students she could see working in the distance.

"I'm afraid not. But thank you for your help."

"Anytime," she heard one of them say as she made her way back to the car and drove the long length of packed dirt. One drop, then another spattered her windshield. It wouldn't be long before the parking area turned into a mud bog.

The closer she drew to Alik's temporary home, the faster her pulse raced. She could hear the blood pounding in her ears.

In the field, Alik's day always started at dawn. It was possible he was already out on the site. She'd left the Bluebird Inn in Warwick at five-thirty in the morning, hoping to catch him before he began measuring soil properties or mapping water resources.

During the Introduction to Geology class she'd taken from the fascinating guest lecturer at UCLA in San Diego, California, a year ago, she'd learned he did a myriad of scientific disciplines in his study of the earth. But those all-too-short talks before and after class hadn't been enough for Blaire. She'd fallen deeply in love with the ruggedly attractive Easterner after he'd taken her home from school because she was sick.

Apparently the brief drive to her house hadn't satisfied his needs, either. Once she'd recovered, he'd suggested they have dinner overlooking the ocean. From that point on they couldn't bear to be separated from each other. After a short courtship filled with romantic late-night walks along the surf, they set the date for their wedding and he flew her to New York City to meet his family.

That was when the horror story started. She'd had

no choice but to break off their engagement. In truth, Blaire had never imagined she would see him again, especially if she allowed herself to think back to the awful blackness of that period.

But something unimaginable had come up, something she needed to talk to him about, otherwise she would never be able to live with herself.

Her mouth went dry as she got out of the car and found the strength to walk through the steady rain to the door of his trailer where she saw a poster mounted. No doubt he'd been forced to make a list of his business hours so the latest group of female students wouldn't lie in wait for him the way they'd done in San Diego.

Was he already involved with one of them?

Stop it, Blaire.

She didn't dare start thinking about what he'd been doing for the last ten and half months, let alone the women he'd been dating. Otherwise pain would consume her alive.

According to the poster, he was available for consultation between four and five in the afternoon, Monday through Friday, unless he was out of town.

Quickly, before she lost her courage and disappeared in the opposite direction, she lifted her hand and knocked on the door. She waited for a minute and knocked again. When there was no answer, she debated what to do, then tried turning the handle. To her surprise, it gave. She leaned her head inside and called out to him.

He wasn't there.

After flying all the way from the West Coast to see him, she intended to talk to him no matter how long it took. Wondering how much her body could take in anticipation of this meeting, she considered waiting for him in her car. But the place where she'd had to park would prevent her from spotting him if he returned.

She vacillated for a moment, then decided to wait for him inside his trailer. He had to come back at some point. If the rain kept up, maybe it would be sooner.

During their courtship, Alik had intimated that when he worked at a site, any trailer would do since he only required the bare necessities. Viewing the drab brown and beige interior of the generic-looking mobile unit made her realize he'd spoken the truth.

At a glance she could see nothing of a personal nature to tell her about the man who inhabited these claustrophobic premises. After moving a pile of notebooks from a chair, she sat down to wait.

Much as she would have liked to explore his bedroom, she didn't have the right. In fact by entering his abode uninvited, he could accuse her of trespassing.

Blaire had no idea how he would react when he saw the liberty she'd taken. But with the rain falling harder now, surely she could be forgiven for seeking shelter.

After a few minutes she got up to stretch her legs and discovered a huge map of the U.S. spread out on the built-in table next to the tiny kitchen. Curious, she made her way through the obstacle course to look at it.

He'd drawn a pencil line from New York City to San Francisco. Over the line he'd applied various colors of magic marker like a continuous patchwork between the cities he'd circled in black: Warwick,

New York; Laramie, Wyoming; Tooele, Utah; San Francisco, California. There was no color beyond Tooele, just the line. Above each color he'd made scientific notations she didn't understand.

Intrigued, she wasn't aware of anything until the door was flung wide and she felt footsteps shake the floor. Suddenly Alik's six-foot-two-physique dwarfed the interior of the trailer. The door closed behind him.

Blaire didn't know who was more surprised, but where she let out a quiet gasp before straightening, his bronzed, whipcord-lean body stilled in place. The incandescent blaze in those forest-green eyes was the only part of him that let her know he wasn't an inanimate block of quarry marble.

Through lashes as black as his overly long hair dampened by the rain, his gaze scorched its way up her silken-clad legs. Swallowing hard, she felt it skim the flare of womanly hips beneath her skirt. After a breathless pause, it wandered over the generous curves filling out her cotton sweater. When their eyes met again, she was quivering like a heavy dewdrop on a fragile petal.

"I couldn't begin to guess why you're here," his voice rasped, "but you know the way out." After opening the door, he stood there with his arms folded across his chest.

She'd imagined this meeting in her mind a thousand times at least, but nothing could have prepared her to deal with the extent of his deep-seated rancor.

He despised her.

"Alik—" His stance was so intimidating, she smoothed a lock of auburn hair behind her ear nervously. As she did so, his eye must have caught the glint of the diamond on her ring finger. The skin around his compelling male mouth seemed to whiten.

"I—I can understand how angry you must be finding me here like this," she began in a shaky voice. "But it was raining, and I was afraid I might miss you if I stayed in the car, so I—"

"Get out of here, Blaire." He didn't shout the words. They were muttered beneath his breath like a curse.

She reeled from the raw brutality of his demand. The man she would always love had changed into someone she didn't know.

No matter that she'd broken off their engagement for reasons he must never learn about, she couldn't have imagined him treating her, or anyone else, with such exquisite cruelty. His capacity to inflict pain was a revelation.

"I'll go," she whispered, "just as soon as I tell you there were consequences the night we slept together."

A palpable tension filled the devastating silence of the trailer. He shut the door, then leaned against it.

Gathering her courage she said, "We have a son who was born on August 19th. He's six weeks old, and was christened Nicholas Regan Jarman."

Next to telling him she couldn't marry him, this was the hardest thing she'd ever had to do in her life. But now that she'd started, she had to see it through.

"You have every right to know you're a father, especially since I'm being married in two months and another man will be raising him."

It was a lie. There was no other man. There never could be another man. But it was imperative Alik believe she was engaged to someone else. Blaire's aunt had let her borrow the ring she was wearing. She was on a precarious mission and needed it to authenticate her untruth.

The white around his mouth spread to his face. *The look of shock.*

"I happen to believe this kind of news should be delivered in person," she continued. "Certainly you deserve that. But until Nicky and I both had our checkups yesterday, I wasn't able to travel."

The sardonic slash of his black brows told her exactly what he thought of her fabrication. He moved away from the door and took a threatening step toward her.

The motion drew her attention to the white T-shirt covering his well-defined chest, the powerful thigh muscles visible beneath his jeans. His utter maleness overwhelmed her. It had been so long since she'd lain against him while they'd kissed each other senseless.

"If you had wanted me to believe this fantastic story, you would have brought the proof with you surely."

His biting mockery cut her like a knife. She sucked in her breath. "I would have, but he's your mirror image. Since I'm positive no one around here knows about me or our past relationship, I tried to respect your privacy by leaving him with the hotel sitter. That way I wouldn't embarrass you. Not even the two male students who pointed out your trailer to me know who I am."

His withering look sent her to the door.

So far she hadn't broken down, but if she remained another few seconds, the tears would gush and there wouldn't be any way to stop them.

"What you do with the information is up to you,

Alik. I'm staying at the Bluebird Inn in Warwick until checkout time at eleven tomorrow morning. I——If you want to see your little boy,'' she stammered, ''I'll wait for you that long.''

After shutting the door quietly, she dashed to her rental car, but couldn't escape a good soaking by the rain. She didn't expect Alik to come after her, but some habits died hard as she watched for him through the rearview mirror until the trailer disappeared from her sight.

Fear had warred with excitement over seeing him again. The tension had made her body so twitchy, her foot wouldn't stay on the pedal. She took a deep breath and willed herself to calm down.

You did it, Blaire. You told him the truth. No matter if you were taking an enormous risk, it was the honorable thing to do. Now it's done.

By the time she reached the outskirts of Warwick, the rain had turned to drizzle. She lowered the speed of the windshield wipers. At least she could see better than before.

Yesterday she'd left San Diego under sunny skies. Only a mission as vital as this could have forced her to fly a second time to New York where she'd experienced the greatest pain of her life.

She hated it here, and couldn't wait to get back to California with her darling baby. As soon as she reached the hotel, she would confirm her reservation for the return trip home tomorrow afternoon.

Finally the Bluebird Inn came into view. Anxious to hold Nicky and make sure he was all right, she pulled around the back and entered through a door located close to her hotel room on the second floor.

It hadn't been easy to leave him with a complete

stranger, but the manager of the Inn had assured her the baby-sitter was a retired registered nurse with impeccable credentials. There'd never been one complaint about her in the three years she'd worked for them.

Though it had frightened her, Blaire had been forced to trust the older woman with her most priceless possession. The visit to the site had only required that Blaire be gone two hours at the most, but it had still been a hard thing to do when she'd never been separated from Nicky before.

For several reasons, she realized it wouldn't have been fair to spring the baby on Alik from out of the blue.

Certainly she hadn't wanted to arouse any suspicion in the students and staff at the site. But more importantly, Alik needed time to absorb the earth-shaking news that he had fathered a son. Only time would tell if his hatred of her overshadowed the desire to see the child of his own flesh.

Alik was a man of strong passions and convictions. He was also one of the most honorable men she'd ever known. No matter how bitter his feelings toward her, he wouldn't have received the news she'd just given him lightly.

But they hadn't been together in almost a year. Since she'd broken their engagement, there would have been many changes in the interim. For one thing, he wasn't on the university guest lecture circuit.

At this point in time she knew nothing about the nature of his present project, let alone his state of mind.

Unbearable as she found the idea, he might be in

a serious relationship with another woman. *Even married,* a tiny voice whispered.

If he had a wife, Blaire couldn't begin to imagine how news of a baby from a former relationship would affect him or his marriage.

The more she went over the imponderables in her heart, the more she knew she'd done the right thing by preparing him first.

And if he didn't come to see his son?

Her hand went to her throat.

If he didn't come, then it meant that after weighing everything very carefully, he'd decided that never setting eyes on his tiny offspring was for the best. If that were the case, she'd already made up her mind never to question that decision.

The most important thing was, she'd given him the opportunity to know of Nicky's existence, and could leave with a clear conscience. Tomorrow she would board the plane with her baby, having said a final farewell to the past.

Nicky was the love of her life now, her future. He would be the constant reminder of Alik and the great love they'd once shared. She would devote every waking moment to being the best mother a child could ever have.

She tapped on the hotel room door before unlocking it so as not to alarm the sitter. To her relief, she found the woman sitting in a chair holding the baby against her shoulder.

''Mrs. Wood? How's Nicky? Has he cried for his bottle?''

The older woman smiled. ''He barely woke up and has been a perfect little gentleman. Such a sweet nature for a big boy. I was hoping you would be gone longer. There's nothing like a newborn, especially this one. With his dark curly hair and beautiful olive skin, his father must be as handsome as blazes."

Blaire cleared her throat. "He is."

"Makes me baby hungry for more grandchildren."

"I can't thank you enough."

"Say no more. I know exactly how you feel. When it's your first child, you're almost afraid to breathe, let alone be out of its sight."

"Am I that transparent?"

She chuckled as she handed the baby to Blaire. "A new mother with her baby is a wonderful thing to behold. I'm glad I could be of help."

"So am I."

Blaire took fifty dollars from her purse and pressed it in the woman's hand.

"Oh, no, my dear. That's twenty too much."

"If it hadn't been absolutely necessary, I would never have left my baby at all. To know you were watching after him settled my mind a great deal. Please keep it with my heartfelt thanks."

"Thank you." She patted Blaire's arm, then gave the baby a kiss on the top of his head before leaving the room.

After locking the door, Blaire rocked Nicky in her arms. "Oh, you feel good. Have you missed me as much as I missed you?" She covered his face with kisses.

"I bet by the time I order an early lunch and it's delivered to the room, you'll be hungry for your bottle. Come with mommy."

She walked over to the phone at the bedside table and called for a meal to be sent up. Since boarding the plane yesterday she'd had no appetite. But now that the miracle had happened and she'd found Alik, talked to him, she was hungry.

While she waited for the food to arrive, she gave Nicky a sponge bath and dressed him in his blue stretchy suit with feet. By now he was making sounds that he was hungry for his next feeding.

Thank heaven for prepared formula she could empty right from a can into his bottle. He was such a good baby, he didn't even mind it at room temperature.

She lay down on the bed and fed him in the crook of her arm. He'd been blessed with a healthy appetite. While he devoured the contents, she studied every detail of his precious face and body, which had measured twenty-two inches long when he was born.

He not only had Alik's skin and coloring, but one day he would grow to be tall like his father. Having just come from seeing Alik, Blaire could pick out the many characteristics that already made Nicky recognizable as one of *the* beautiful, fabulously wealthy Jarmans of Long Island, a well-established, well-connected banking family on both sides of the ocean.

The whole clan had exceptional good looks, especially Alik's mother, a physically beautiful woman with luxuriant black hair reminiscent of her Greek ancestry. Alik resembled her the most in appearance. *But not in anything else, thank heaven.* His height he'd inherited from his dark-blond, green-eyed father who'd come from English parentage.

Nicky's Regan genes seemed to have contributed more to his even temperament. He'd inherited a sunny disposition for which Blaire's mother was famous. So far his eyes were a cloudy color. Perhaps Blaire had given him her gray eyes. Only time would tell.

*   *   *

There'd been several knocks on the door of the trailer since Blaire's hasty exit, but Alik had ignored them. The drone of the rain on the roof was driving him mad. He tossed down his second scotch, but the hoped-for state of oblivion hadn't occurred yet. Maybe if he finished off the whole bottle a miracle would happen and he would pass out.

Until Blaire had ripped his heart from his body almost a year ago, he'd rarely drunk anything more than an occasional beer or glass of wine. Since their excruciating breakup for which she offered some mumbo jumbo explanation about him being too old for her after all, he'd kept something stronger on hand for emergencies—like those times in the middle of the night when the emotional wound oozed more blood and the pain got so bad he needed relief.

This was one of those moments, only it wasn't even noon. Damn her to hell for showing up with such an improbable, ludicrous tale just when the new project had given him a reason to get up in the mornings.

Alik threw the empty tumbler across the expanse. It hit the wall, then ricocheted to the petrographic microscope, shattering both the glass and the lens. The fact that he'd caused damage to an expensive tool of his trade didn't faze him.

He could still see her mouth forming the words. That luscious red mouth he helplessly devoured over and over in dreams he hadn't been able to control.

We have a son who was born August 19th. He's six weeks old and was christened Nicholas Regan Jarman.

He actually had a son she called Nicky? A child from his own loins? Alik shook his dark head. *Dear God.* Could she possibly be telling the truth?

You have every right to know you're a father, especially because I'm being married in two months and another man will be raising him.

Full of rage, Alik leaped to his feet, kicking a couple of geology journals out of the way with the tip of his boot. Did Blaire take him for a complete fool, one who would lie down and die for her? Is that what she really thought?

No doubt her latest fiancé was the man who'd made her pregnant, the one for whom she'd dumped Alik while he'd been out of town giving a geological seminar in Kentucky.

Now that the baby was born, the bastard didn't want anything to do with it. He'd probably threatened to withhold financial support, so she'd decided to fob it off as Alik's love child, hoping he would kick in with the funds.

Like hell!

He reached for the uncapped bottle and made his way through the cluttered trailer to his bedroom. But he couldn't get away from her last salvo reverberating in his head.

I'm staying at the Bluebird Inn in Warwick until checkout time at eleven tomorrow morning. If you want to see your little boy, I'll wait for you that long.

His bitterness had reached its zenith. He lifted the bottle to his lips. "You can wait until hell freezes over, my beloved," he ground out before draining what was left.

Oblivion meant you never had to wake up. Unfortunately Alik's respite from pain lasted only as long as the phone didn't ring.

Disoriented because it was so dark in the room, he ran a hand over the stubble on his jaw and tried to sit up. The room spun. He felt like the devil, but the damn phone continued to jar his nerves.

Through bleary eyes he checked his watch. It was quarter to eight? He fell back against the pillow from dizziness. That meant he'd been passed out for ten hours.

What did he expect after drinking a bottle of scotch on an empty stomach!

His cell phone was in the other room. Who in the hell would let it ring twenty times?

Blaire. That's who. She was desperate for money. Too bad she hadn't figured out which side her bread was buttered on before she'd betrayed him with another man.

They'd only slept together once—the night before he'd had to leave to give that emergency seminar. From the beginning, he'd held off making love to her until after their marriage because he knew she was a virgin.

But something about his going away on that last unexpected trip had made her so insecure, she'd begged him to take her to bed, assuring him that her OB had put her on the pill at her premarital checkup. It had never occurred to him not to believe her.

At that point in time he'd been too seduced by her warmth and beauty, too deeply in love, too filled with desire for her to see what was coming.

The night they'd made love was the last time he would ever see her again.

Until this morning...

If she'd lied to him about the pill, then the baby could be anybody's. As far as Alik was concerned, if he had fathered her child, then he wanted DNA proof of his paternity!

Staggering off the bed, he groped his way to the shower and let the water pour over his head until it cleared enough that he could make it to the kitchen without falling down.

The thought of a meal sounded repulsive, but he toasted a slice of bread to put something substantial in his stomach. Two cups of coffee later, he realized that if he didn't bite the bait, he would always have a question in his mind about the real reason for her unprecedented visit.

Much as he dreaded the idea of seeing her again, of being in the same room with the only woman who'd ever held such fatal appeal for him, he couldn't live with this thing left unresolved. Not if he wanted to survive the rest of his life.

Obviously he'd never known the real Blaire. It seemed she'd been a bewitching liar all along, deceitfully drawing him down to hell with silken cords fashioned expressly for him. But his instincts told him she wasn't lying about the existence of a baby.

All that remained was to call her bluff. Then he could write Finished to the end of the script and toss it in the trash along with every bittersweet memory.

After brushing his teeth, he dressed in clean trousers and a polo shirt, then left the trailer.

"Dr. Jarman? Wait up!"

His head swam as he turned it. He held on to the door handle to regain his equilibrium. "Hello, Ms. Call. What can I do for you?" The attractive blond graduate student was starting to make a nuisance of herself.

"I've been trying to reach you on the phone. It's Friday night. A whole bunch of us are getting together in Peter's trailer for a party. They elected me to invite you.''

''That's very nice of everyone but I'm afraid I have other plans.''

Not to be daunted she said, ''The party will probably go all night. You'll be welcome whenever you get back.''

''Don't think I'm not appreciative of the invitation, but I haven't partied in years and have no intention of starting now. Good night, Ms. Call.''

She followed him to his truck. ''Why won't you call me Sandy?''

''I never address female students by their first names on the job.'' He got inside and shut the door.

''What about off the job?'' she asked in a surprisingly brazen manner through the open window.

''There is no 'off the job' when it comes to students.''

The only time he'd broken that rule had been with Blaire. It had turned out to be the greatest mistake of his life. He had an idea he would spend the rest of eternity paying for it. Tonight was a case in point.

He backed away, then floored the accelerator, almost hoping the dust flew in the aggressive Ms. Call's face so she would get the point. With Blaire it had been the other way around. He'd done all the running. Until she'd let him catch her…

She'd missed his first test and had called his office with an excuse that she'd gotten the flu and didn't feel well enough to take the exam. Used to the wiles of some of the female students who traded on their good looks for favors, he didn't believe her and told her to come into his office. He'd give her the exam orally if she couldn't write.

The breathtaking, auburn-haired student ten to twelve years his junior who'd shown up for the appointment did indeed have the flu. She appeared unsteady on her feet and the red stains on her cheeks were due to a fever.

Without conscious thought he put the back of his hand to the skin of her cheek where her shoulder-length hair had been swept aside. It was hot to the touch. At the slight contact, surprised dove-gray eyes fringed by black lashes fused with his. In that moment he felt a quickening pass through both their bodies.

"Forgive me for not believing you," he whispered, lowering his hand. "When did you notice the flu coming on?"

"This morning."

He sucked in his breath. "You must feel wretched and should be home in bed. How did you drive here in this condition?"

"I took the bus."

Scandalized by his insensitive treatment of her over the phone earlier, he said, "This is my fault. I'm through lecturing for today and will drive you home."

"Oh, no." She shook her head. "That's very kind of you, but it won't be necessary. As long as I'm here, please let me take the test, then I'll go."

Though he could sense her reservations about being alone with him, he knew a fire had been lit inside her. The same fire had been ignited inside him when he'd touched her skin. An invisible energy crackled between them.

Her breathing had grown shallow. A tiny pulse in the scented hollow of her throat throbbed out of control. He had an irresistible urge to press his mouth to it.

"Forget the test. I'll drive you home."

"My parents' house is twelve miles away from campus. That's too far. I couldn't let you do it."

The more she retreated, the more determined he was to have his way.

"If you won't allow me to make amends, then I'll call for a taxi."

"Please no. I don't have the cash on me."

"Naturally I would pay."

Her small gasp of frustration pleased him. "Dr. Jarman—"

"The name is Alik. If you're going to refuse all help, then let me call one of your parents to come and get you."

"My dad's the only one with a car and he teaches at a junior high. I wouldn't dream of getting him out of class."

He put his hands on his hips. "Then the only thing to do is accompany you home on the bus."

He watched her swallow nervously. "Why would you do that?"

"Because flu can cause a person to pass out. If you start to feel lightheaded, I want to be there with my cell phone to call 911. Admit you're about ready to collapse."

Tears moistened her eyes. "I—I admit it," she stammered.

Through with this nonsense, he walked over to the door and turned out the light. "Come on. My car's right outside the back steps of the building. I'm taking you home. Now."

In those last seconds of hesitation, he knew she was fighting more than her desire not to be a burden.

His world changed the moment she moved past him

in acquiescence. Like a lick of flame, the accidental brush of her hip against his sealed his fate.

As the sign for Warwick came into view, Alik's torturous thoughts returned to the present with a jerk.

A long time ago he'd consigned Blaire Regan to the devil. Such a beautiful, treacherous coward, she'd ended their love affair long distance proffering no explanation he could live with. To compound the pain, she'd run away where he couldn't find her. By refusing to face him, her cruel actions had denied him any possibility of permanent closure.

His jaw hardened.

She'd made a fatal mistake by daring to show up at his trailer this morning. Before the night was out she would learn the definition of cruelty. Then it would be she who rued the day their paths had ever crossed.

The knuckles of his hand gleamed white as he turned the steering wheel to enter the parking area in front of the Bluebird Inn.

CHAPTER TWO

WITH the bulk of the ten o'clock television news coverage over, Blaire realized she'd been waiting for something that was never going to happen.

She looked down at her adorable baby who was still wide-awake on one of the double beds, almost as if he knew this day and night had been different from all the others. His fingers clung to her pinky.

"How sad Alik's never going to know you, my little love." One salty tear dropped, then another. "You have no idea what a wonderful man he is, Nicky. There's no one his equal, except for you. I pray you'll grow up to be exactly like him."

She used the edge of the baby quilt she'd made for him to wipe her eyes. "I'm not talking about the angry man I confronted this morning. I'm afraid that man is the result of what I did to him. He'll never forgive me, I can see that now. Why should he? If he'd done the same thing to me, I'm not sure I'd even be alive.

"When he walked in his trailer this morning and saw me, he had every right to throw me out bodily. But he didn't. He could have called me a liar. In fact he could have called me every cruel name he could think of. He could have shouted loud enough for everyone at the site to hear him. Yet he restrained himself, because he's a real man."

The lump lodged in her throat refused to move. "I did an awful thing to him, Nicky. I hurt him the worst way you can hurt a man. It destroyed me, too. But I had no choice. None…''

She leaned over to kiss the top of his nose. Every time she looked at his precious face, it was Alik all over again. Just in miniature.

''I believe it was destiny the day I came down with that bout of flu in college. I was already halfway in love with your father, the brilliant, famous, drop-dead gorgeous Dr. Jarman. Every woman in class had fantasies about him. Yet I was the lucky one who had to go to his office to take my test.

''He was unbelievably tender with me.'' A delicious shiver ran through her as she relived the feel of his hand on her face to check her temperature. ''After driving me home, he brought me dinner and flowers. I didn't have to take the test until I was better. By then I so madly in love with him, I forgot I had any other classes.

''We spent every waking moment together. Most evenings we walked along the beach talking about our lives, then ended up in each other's arms. He shared his dreams with me. Imagine. *Me.* I told him mine. You were part of those dreams, Nicky. You and the rest of the family we were going to rear one day.

''Your father has led such a fascinating life. His privileged background has given him the best education in the best schools. He's gone on adventures that have taken him all over the world. What's so amazing about all this is that he became my world, and I became his.

''Though I was forced to break up with him—'' her voice shook in remembered pain of that ghastly time when he was away giving a seminar ''—I'll always be thankful he made me pregnant with you.

You're all I have left of him. When we get home, I'm never looking back again. What I am going to do is raise you to be the same, magnificent man he is. I plan to devote my life to you, my sweet love.

"Come on. Let's get you undressed and ready for bed. We have a long flight home to San Diego tomorrow. You need your sleep. So do I."

As she got up from the bed to find his nightgown in the diaper bag, the phone rang. The baby's arms flailed in the air.

That would be Blaire's mother calling to find out how things had gone today.

Not so well, Mom.

Blaire walked around to the bedside table to pick up the receiver and said hello.

"Ms. Regan? This is the front desk. There's a Dr. Jarman here who said you were expecting him."

The receiver slipped from her fingers. It clanked against the wood. With trembling hands she grasped for it.

"Y-yes. I am. Please send him up."

Dear God.

"Very good."

After hearing the click, she replaced the receiver and dashed to the bathroom to retouch her lipstick. Her hair needed a good brushing after playing with the baby who had started to reach for the strands. She probably ought to cut it, but it was too thick to wear short.

The blue cotton sweater and designer jeans she'd chosen to wear no longer seemed right, but it was too late now. She could hear his familiar tap on the door. He didn't do it like anyone else. Her heart skipped a beat. Some things never changed.

She hurried out of the bathroom toward the door to the hotel room. But she was so frightened and excited all at the same time, she had to stop and try to pull herself together before she opened it.

This morning Alik had been breathtaking enough in a T-shirt and jeans. Tonight he was shaven and dressed in a navy polo shirt and cargo pants, the kind of clothes that revealed his devastating masculinity. He put every other man to shame.

Embarrassed because she'd been feasting her eyes, she quickly lifted her gaze to his face, fearful of seeing the same chilling look in his green eyes he'd directed at her earlier in the day. But for once something else had caught his attention. He stared past her shoulder to the baby still dressed in his adorable yellow suit who happened to be in Alik's direct line of vision.

She noticed the sharp rise and fall of his chest before he swept past her in a few long strides to reach the bed. In his haste, he'd forgotten to shut the door. Blaire closed it, then walked slowly toward him waiting for his reaction.

With that effortless male grace, which was unconscious on his part, he sank down on the bed next to the baby. Her breath caught as she watched him lean over Nicky and run a hand through his curly black hair.

Their son didn't seem particularly disturbed that a total stranger had started to undress him. Nicky's sweet temperament allowed Alik to examine every part of his anatomy, from his broad shoulders to his square-tipped fingers and long legs without making a fuss.

While he lay there looking up at his father with

cloudy eyes already fringed by long black lashes like Alik's, his dark male beauty and olive skin, the square jaw, the way his shell ears lay close to his perfectly shaped head, all screamed Jarman.

"Dear Lord— I have a son."

The reverence, the wonder in Alik's husky tone told Blaire how much this moment meant to him. Her heart swelled until she thought it might burst. No matter if she'd done everything else wrong in life, she'd done this one thing right.

Clearing her throat she murmured, "Perhaps now you'll understand why I didn't dare bring him to the site. People would have taken one look at him an—"

"Why didn't you tell me you were pregnant?" he demanded before she could finish. The tender side had disappeared as if it had never been.

By now Alik had gathered their near-naked baby against his shoulder with the quilt. He rose to his full, intimidating height.

She backed away from the fury in his glittering gaze. "I—I didn't know I was pregnant when I broke our engagement. After I found out, I thought it better not to tell you."

"Why? Damn you." He hadn't raised his voice. Maybe that's why his excoriating rebuke sounded more deadly.

Clasping her hands together she said, "I told you I had been put on birth control pills, but the doctor said I should have been on them a full month b-before—"

"That still doesn't explain why I wasn't informed you were carrying my son." His voice grated.

Aghast at his unexpected anger, she struggled for

words that would appease him. Anything but the truth.

"I knew how much you hated me for ending our relationship the way I did. There was no excuse for my unconscionable behavior. I realize I was a coward. It's because I was too immature for a man like you. Under the circumstances, I didn't want to bring any more grief to your life."

His features hardened, making him appear older than his thirty-six years.

"If that's the case, then why in the hell have you come here now?"

She fought to hold back the sobs for the bitterness and hurt in his voice.

I'm so sorry for what I've done to you, my darling. You'll never know the nightmare I've lived through. I can never tell you.

"Because having a baby forced me to consider someone else besides myself. Before Nicky's delivery, it was all still like a dream. But when the doctor laid him across my stomach, I was struck with the realization that he was half yours. In that moment I determined that as soon as my OB would allow me to travel, I would bring him to you.

"I couldn't have lived with myself if I'd kept this knowledge from you. As the father of our baby, it's your God-given right to know he exists. R-Rick agrees."

"Rick?" The skin around Alik's mouth had gone a bluish-white. If she didn't know better, she would think he were ill.

"Rick Hammond, my fiancé." *Dear God, the lies...* "He knows I'm here, and he knows why. After we're married, he intends to be a wonderful father to

Nicky. Rick's a good person. You can trust him to help me raise our son.''

A stillness had come over Alik. It should have warned her to stop talking, but she'd been working on this speech for weeks and needed to get it all said while she still had the courage.

''I—If you want to see Nicky from time to time, I'm willing to work out visitation with you. I'll give you my phone number.'' She moved over to the counter by the television and wrote it down on a piece of hotel stationery. ''After Rick and I are married, I'll let you know my new one.''

As she lifted her head, she noticed he'd put the baby back down on the bed. To her shock, he'd stretched out beside Nicky and was testing the strength of their little boy's hands and arms.

The deep chuckle that came out of Alik testified to his delight in his offspring. Many times she'd dreamed about a domestic scene like this between father and son, but the reality was so poignant, she found herself fighting tears again.

''Alik?'' His actions made her wonder if he'd even heard her.

''What is it?'' he asked without looking in her direction.

''I know all of this has come as a tremendous shock. You don't need to make up your mind about visitation tonight. If you need time to decide what you want to do, I'll certainly understand.''

''I don't need time,'' came the blunt reply. ''I want custody of Nicky.''

It was her turn to freeze in place. Surely she hadn't heard him correctly.

Calm down, Blaire. He's only baiting you because

he has to go somewhere with all the anger that's been bottled up inside him for the past year. Don't take anything he says seriously. He looks exhausted. In a few minutes he'll leave and that will be the end of it.

Pretending she hadn't heard him, she found the baby's nightgown in the diaper bag, then walked over to pick up Nicky and put him in the crib. But by this time Alik had nestled the baby against his shoulder with one strong, suntanned hand spanning his little back.

"I need to get him ready for bed, Alik."

He stared up at her, his slumberous gaze narrowed on her features. "I need time to get acquainted with my son. There are two double beds in here. You look tired. Why don't you go to sleep in the other one. I'll take care of him."

"Don't be absurd!" she cried before remembering that she wasn't going to let him get to her.

"I see you brought cans of formula with you." He spoke in a conversational tone, ignoring her outburst. "Did you do that so I could feed him, or aren't you nursing?"

The intimate question caught her off guard because she hadn't expected him to think about things like that. She found herself blushing. Her reaction was ridiculous considering the fact that they'd spent a whole night making love. That night the term "one flesh" took on a whole new meaning, with Nicky as the final result.

"I nursed him in the hospital, but he developed a serious rash. The pediatrician told me he's allergic to my milk, so I switched to formula. I use something different when I'm home, but the canned milk works fine for travel."

Not being able to nurse had come as a huge disappointment to her. But compared to the more serious problems some mothers faced with their newborns, she had no room to complain.

"In that case I'll be able to give him his next feeding. If you can't go to sleep with the light on, by all means turn it off. Nicky and I will get along just fine in the dark, won't we, son."

This game had gone far enough. She sat down on the bed opposite him, unaware she was torturing the nightgown in her hands. Preoccupied with an animated Nicky and his baby noises, Alik refused to look at her.

"It's getting late." She had to think fast. "I promised Rick I would phone him before I went to bed."

"Go ahead. So far our son's behavior has been perfect. This is probably the best time to talk. Rick needs to know that I'm not relinquishing my right to raise Nicky. On the contrary, I plan to father him on a full-time basis from here on out."

The finality in his tone terrified Blaire. She bowed her head.

"You can't do that. He's my son, too, Alik."

"I'm afraid you should have thought of that before you entered my trailer without being invited. If you think I'm going to allow him to be raised by another man who answers to Daddy, and calls him son, then you never knew me, and I sure as hell never knew you. Except of course for one night in the biblical sense," he scathed, wounding her in new ways that went marrow deep.

She slid off the edge of the bed and got to her feet, too upset to remain in one position. "Why don't you go home and get a good night's sleep. I'll do the same. In the morning we'll be fresh and can talk over breakfast before I have to leave for the airport with Nicky."

His answer was to place the baby on his stomach and rub the back of his head in a soothing motion. While Nicky lay there perfectly content, Blaire felt like screaming.

"I know you're angry, Alik. You have every right to be. But please let's not fight over Nicky. He's an innocent baby who deserves the best from both of us. As long as you want to be a part of his life, I'm willing to work out something reasonable with you."

His piercing glance trapped hers. "I plan to be very reasonable. How much do you want in order to give me exclusive parental rights? Two million dollars? Three? What's your price? Why not talk it over with Rick. I'm willing to negotiate as long as he names a figure that's somewhere in the ball park."

She shook her head in exasperation. "My baby is not for sale at any price."

His mocking smile shattered her. "A little while ago you hastened to inform me he was *our* baby."

"Stop it, Alik!"

"You started it by coming to New York and presenting me with our little fait accompli.

"Did you think I was going to forgive your crimes because you decided at the midnight hour to do the decent thing in letting me know I was a father?" Rage had made the cords stand out in his neck.

"We have a son. He isn't a piece of property to be passed back and forth when the mood suits either one of us. Nicky's beautiful. Perfect. I've been cheated out of his first six weeks.

"It's obvious you never loved me. Because you

couldn't bring yourself to marry me, I was denied the thrill of watching him grow inside you over the nine months you were pregnant. That's not something I'm going to forget. But it's in the past.

"All that matters now is that I love him. I plan to fight for him, Blaire. I know I can win. I have friends in high places, and I have the kind of money it takes to get what I want.

"I hope I've made it clear I want my son. When you call Rick, you tell him that for me. No matter how accommodating he's been, let's be honest. If he's any kind of a man, he'll prefer making his own babies with you.

"Here!" He reached in his trouser pocket and tossed his cell phone on the other bed. "Be my guest. Since I'm planning to stay the night, you'll need to go in the bathroom and shut the door if you don't want me to overhear your conversation.

"Before you go, toss me that nightgown and I'll get this little tyke ready for bed. He just gave me a huge yawn, which reminds me how sleepy I am. This has been quite a day for both of us, hasn't it, son."

She struggled for breath. "You can't stay here, Alik!"

"What are you worried about? I'm certainly not about to leap on an unwilling woman who left me and ran away because she couldn't stand the sight of me. Remind Rick of that fact when he tells you he doesn't approve of your spending the night in the same room with me.

"Of course if it's a case of *your* sensibilities being offended now that you're wearing his ring, you're welcome to book another room for yourself. I'll pay for it."

Suffused by the white-hot heat of anger she cried, "I thought by doing the honorable thing that you—"

"No—" He broke in brutally. "You never thought about anyone but Blaire Regan. I suspect Rick is a good deal younger than I am, and doesn't have a dime to his name. He's probably panting to get you into bed if he hasn't already, and is praying I'll come through with enough child support to set you up."

"How dare you!"

But those very words crucified her even as she said them because Alik had every right to be in a rage. The damage she'd done to him by breaking their engagement was so much worse than she'd supposed. And now she was forced to perpetuate a lie about a fiancé who didn't exist. All because she'd wanted Alik to know he had a son. *What have I done?*

If he fought for custody, his family would get involved. After all his mother had threatened, if she were to find out it was Blaire's child...

Blaire shuddered, not even wanting to think about that because Alik's mother would *never* accept Nicky as a Jarman. The knowledge of his existence would create such enmity between Alik and his family, it would turn into a living horror story.

In the end Alik and Nicky would be the ones who were destroyed. She couldn't do that to them. She couldn't let it happen. Right now she needed the wisdom of Solomon to know where to turn, how to stop the precarious situation from escalating.

Feeling physically and emotionally ill, she turned out the light and sank down on top of the other bed to think. But the hopelessness of this nightmare overwhelmed her. Turning her back to Alik, she buried her face in the pillow to stifle her sobs.

After a few minutes, "Once upon a time those tears might have moved me," came the gravelly male voice out of the darkness. "To have the thing you prized most in life snatched away without warning is a life-changing experience, isn't it, Blaire? I have to say it's one you've been long overdue.

"Do you know I used to lie awake nights planning different ways I would exact my revenge to make you suffer even one-hundredth of my pain? Little did I know that one day down the road, you would appear in my trailer to supply me with the perfect instrument to inflict that torture back on you."

Unable to bear the stinging pain any longer, she drew herself upright, smoothing the hair out of her tear-ravaged face.

"Consider your revenge complete, Alik. I'm prepared to grovel because I can't lose Nicky. He's my life!"

"You mean Rick isn't?"

This was one time she had to be totally honest. "Not in the same way."

"The poor, stupid devil. You're the kind of woman who needs to wear a warning sign, Love Me At Your Own Peril."

Every thrust of his rapier tongue ripped apart what little of her heart his family had left intact. Now there was nothing more to shred.

"Name your price," she said in wooden voice. "Just promise me you won't bring the courts into it and sue me for full custody of Nicky." *Please don't do that or your family will find out.* "I—I'd rather be dead."

A long, tension-filled silence ensued. The baby

must have fallen asleep in his Alik's arms. She hadn't heard a peep out of him.

"That's an interesting proposition," he muttered silkily. "Let me think about it. I'll give you my answer in the morning." The sound of satisfaction in his tone made her tremble.

While both the baby and Alik slept, she spent the next three hours in a frantic state of torment trying to figure out what his answer would involve. The only possibility that made sense would be if he demanded she live in the same city so they could share custody.

But if he forced her to do that, then her bogus story about a fiancé would be exposed. There was no way on earth she could come up with a fake husband-to-be. It meant she would have to concoct another story about Rick not wanting to leave San Diego, so they'd decided to call off their engagement.

She could hear Alik's mocking words when she informed him of that particular piece of news.

That makes two down, Blaire. How many more to go before the male of the species learns to look, then run for dear life in the opposite direction.

By the time Nicky started making hungry sounds, she'd come to terms with the fact that she might have to move to Warwick and rent an apartment until Alik's work took him elsewhere. But whatever she had to do, it was worth it to keep her baby.

As for Alik's parents, they still wouldn't have to know anything about his secret child. Thank heaven Long Island was too far away to pose any kind of threat of her being seen in this area of the state.

Out of habit, she got up from the bed and flicked on the light switch to pour Nicky's formula into a clean bottle. When she turned around Alik was right behind her, their fussy baby propped against his shoulder.

"I want to feed him. Show me what to do."

He stood too close. She could feel his warmth. The familiar brand of the soap he used in the shower emanated from his bronzed skin, assailing her senses. His shuttered eyes reminded her of the way he used to look at her when his passion had been aroused.

Out of self-preservation she ran for the baby bag. "He needs to have his diaper changed first," she called over her shoulder. "Lay him down on the quilt and you can do it."

The next few minutes were instructive as he followed her directions with methodical attention to detail. Dr. Jarman was known as a perfectionist. He would be that way when it came to caring for his son.

Out of the periphery she saw the glow in his eyes, revealing the bursting pride in his little boy who was perfect in every way, shape and form.

When he'd finally managed to slip the baby into a clean shirt and nightgown, she suggested he sit at the head of the bed with Nicky nestled in his left arm.

His daddy had taken a little too long for his liking with all the baby wipes, ointment and powder. Now their son was all worked up and clamored for his food.

Averting her eyes, she placed a clean cloth over Alik's broad shoulder, careful not to touch him for fear she wouldn't want to stop. Then she handed him the bottle.

"Go ahead and put it in his mouth. He'll do the rest. When he's drunk a third of it, prop him on your shoulder and gently pat his back to get rid of the air bubbles. By the time he has drained the bottle, he'll be fast asleep again. Give him one more burp and then put him in his crib.

"Be sure to lay him on his back before you cover him with his quilt. The doctor says a lot of infant deaths have been prevented by putting them in that position."

She stood for a minute to watch. Nicky searched in frustration for the nipple, but couldn't quite get hold of it.

"Insert it right into his mouth. He's not a fragile piece of crystal."

When Alik did her bidding, the baby started devouring his formula. He drank so fast and furiously, he made loud noises that sounded indecent. Alik's laughter started in his throat and rumbled out to fill the hotel room.

She couldn't help smiling. "As you're discovering, he has your healthy appetite." Before she gave her feelings away, she removed herself to the other bed.

"Do you want me to leave the light on or off?"

"On," he murmured. "I still have trouble believing he's real, let alone that he came from one night's pleasure with you."

The thickness in his tone sent delicious pains through her body.

"I could look at him all night. He has your eyes and eyebrows. It's your mouth in miniature. Even I who am biased because I'm his father, can see he's a living miracle because you're his mother. For a woman who hates my guts, you've given me a priceless treasure."

She winced at the sudden twist of the knife.

"Because of this noble gesture you've made," he said with glaring sarcasm, "I'm prepared to offer you a deal. There'll be no bargaining. You will either accept it, or I'll take Nicky away from you forever.''

Here it comes, Blaire. Her fingernails dug into the quilted bedspread covering the mattress.

"For the next month you'll live in my trailer with me. Separate beds of course. I need that amount of time to get used to my son's routine, and for him to get used to me.

"At the end of the thirty days—*if* you've kept your side of the bargain by staying put to help me establish an unbreakable bond with our innocent child—then and only then will I be willing to talk about joint custody. Otherwise we go to court. I promise you it will be a fight you'll wish you hadn't started," he vowed with a fierceness she'd never heard come out of him before.

"That's it. That's the bargain. If your fiancé doesn't like the idea of being separated from you for a month, that's tough! Compared to nine months deprivation from my unborn child, he damn well has nothing to complain about."

CHAPTER THREE

BLAIRE didn't close her eyes for the rest of the night. To live with Alik for a month in such close quarters was the last thing she'd expected him to demand.

He'd asked the impossible of her!

Unable to quell the frantic beat of her heart since he'd surprised her in his trailer yesterday, she feared being under one roof with him that long would wear out her vital organ before the thirty days were halfway up.

She needed to be made of stone to endure the torture of being around him day and night, sharing everything except a bed. If she'd thought she'd loved him prior to their breakup, those emotions were nothing compared to the feelings she had for him as she watched the care he was giving Nicky for his six in the morning feeding.

Perhaps there was no more beautiful sight than a strong, powerful man nurturing his little baby with so much love. With Alik this wasn't a show of pretense. His delight in their son was a hundred percent genuine. If Blaire hadn't known that deep in her soul, she might not have set out on this precarious mission.

Now that Alik had told her what he was prepared to do, *she* had a decision to make. But she needed to inform her parents before giving him his answer.

While father and son were otherwise occupied, she got off the bed, gathered a fresh change of clothes and headed for the bathroom with his cell phone.

After locking the door, she turned on the water full force, then phoned home. Her mom and dad adored Alik, and were horribly upset when they'd found out why she'd broken her engagement. Though they hadn't approved of her lying to him about her reason for ending it with him, they'd understood her motives and had left it alone.

When she'd informed them she was expecting his baby, they'd insisted she live with them until after it was born. Without their love and support, she had no idea how she would have managed. Since they'd always maintained Alik had the right to know about his child, they'd backed her decision to fly to New York.

But like her, they were shocked by Alik's ultimatum. When she reminded them that his family was worth millions and he could take Nicky away from her, the silence on the phone told its own story. Her parents worshiped their grandson. To lose him would be unthinkable.

No one knew better than Blaire that her parents lived on a fixed income and could never afford a court battle. Neither could she, especially not on the small amount of money she made doing word processing at home for college students who needed their term papers typed.

The best her parents could do was ask her to call them as often as she could, and remind her that she and Nicky still had a home when the month was up. With muffled tears, she thanked them, then hung up and stepped into the shower.

By the time she'd emerged from the bathroom in a clean blouse and jeans, Alik had put Nicky back in the crib and was lounging on the bed like a dangerous panther lying in wait for its prey.

She braced herself to face the inevitable withering comment from him. It wasn't long in coming.

"That must have been some conversation you had with Rick. I hope you warned him that if he sets foot in my trailer at any time in the next thirty days, all bets are off."

In order to carry out this charade to its necessary conclusion, she had to convince Alik she had a fiancé.

Pretending to be enflamed, she wheeled around. "Why do you assume I have decided to accept your bargain?"

He flashed her a sardonic glance. "Because you didn't try to sneak out with Nicky while I was asleep between feedings."

"I wouldn't have gotten very far," she admitted, reaching for the brush to do her hair.

"I'm glad you recognize that fact."

If she'd really been engaged to another man, his smug remark would have made her furious.

"Enough, Alik. You've won. I'll live with you for a month. But it will be easier for me if you leave my fiancé out of the conversation. He may not like this arrangement, but he urged me to accept your conditions because he knows I'll never be happy if I lose Nicky. That's the kind of man he is, so don't say anything more about him." Her voice trembled.

Judging by the way his expression closed up, she'd done a better job of acting than she'd supposed.

"I called for breakfast to be sent up. It should be here any minute. While we're waiting, let's make a list of the things we'll need for our happy home."

She bit her lip. "There isn't much space to work with in your trailer."

"We'll make room. I prefer cozy to palatial."

Alik had never been able to tolerate his parents' ostentatious lifestyle. He found it obscene to flaunt money, and much preferred to do humanitarian kinds of gestures behind the scenes. In that way alone, he was a remarkable man. If she got started on all his wonderful traits, she wouldn't be able to stop.

"Well, obviously we'll need a crib. I can send for the rest of Nicky's clothes."

He made a sound of exasperation. "I doubt a six-week-old baby has an elaborate wardrobe. We'll shop for the items he needs. After your sudden exit from my world, the experience of buying things for my own daughter or son was something I never expected to happen in my lifetime.

"Having spent the night with him, I've discovered I like being a father much more than I had imagined. I want to buy him one of those padded strollers so he can accompany me around the site. I also want to get a swing. Elizabeth has an automated one that puts her to sleep. Nicky will love it."

"Elizabeth?"

"Hmm. Dominic's daughter. She's a little sweetheart."

That was a name Blaire hadn't heard before. Her pulse rate accelerated. Was it a woman he'd become close to? If so, *how* close?

"Who's Dominique?"

"Someone who means mo—just a minute. That's the door. It'll be our food."

Evidently he hadn't been living like a monk.

During their courtship, Blaire had thought she'd been all things to him. It hurt to discover how many ways he'd changed since their breakup.

She feared living with him would be like trying to

survive in a minefield. Every time she took a step, something else would blow up in her face reminding her of the ten and half months he'd had time to grow apart from her.

So where did this Dominique live with her daughter? In one of the trailers at the site? Was she a professor? Blaire groaned at the unpleasant prospect. No woman could be around Alik and want to be just "good friends."

Alik had never given Blaire any reason to be jealous, but she could feel the green-eyed monster tearing away at her fragile defenses right now. If she asked any more questions about the other woman, Alik would pick up on it. A happily engaged woman was supposed to be so in love, she didn't notice anyone else.

If Blaire acted too curious, Alik would become suspicious. He might even figure out there was no fiancé. Blaire couldn't afford to let that happen. She would have to keep her mouth shut.

Already Blaire hated the unseen woman who'd worked her way into Alik's confidence. She especially hated her beautiful name. Obviously she was French. Someone lovely and exotic. Someone who would appeal to Alik in ways Blaire never could. Had he slept with her?

It was a question she couldn't ask Alik. But not knowing the answer was already destroying her. How on earth was she going to live with him for thirty days when it had only been nine hours and already she was a writhing mass of emotions?

The waiter wheeled the cart into the middle of the room before Alik tipped him and he went out again.

"I don't know about you but I'm starving. Shall we eat?"

He set up their breakfast on the round table next to the wall. She saw waffles and sausage, her favorite. His steel-trap memory never forgot anything. For his fare he'd selected scrambled eggs, French toast, bacon, orange juice and coffee.

It was a veritable feast.

Alik consumed his meal with obvious relish. She found she was hungry, too. After a night without sleep, she needed extra energy before taking this monumental step back into his life.

"Why don't you get Nicky ready while I carry everything down to your rental car and check you out. It has an infant seat for him doesn't it?"

"Yes."

"Then we'll use your vehicle to do our errands before we return it to the agency. Where are the keys?"

"In my purse." She put down her fork to find her bag. When Alik took charge, things happened before she could fathom half of what was going on.

Not many men had the ability to switch from bachelor to father in a matter of minutes! That's all the time it had taken for him to bond with Nicky. One look at his darling little carbon copy and he'd switched hats with an ease that would astonish anyone else.

But not Blaire. She knew him too well. As far as she was concerned, he would always be exceptional. Her problem now was that she was supposed to be engaged to another man. She had to force herself not to think about Alik in any other light than Nicky's father.

Of course that would be an impossible task. Every time she pictured him in her mind, let alone glanced at his hard-muscled physique or felt his dynamic presence, her legs wobbled and she felt desire clear to the palms of her hands.

"Does my little guy want to go for a ride?" Alik swept into the room bigger than life and plucked Nicky from the crib where she'd just changed him into a soft, furry one-piece blue suit with feet.

Nicky had always been an easy baby, but even Blaire had to admit she was surprised at his acceptance of Alik who'd been a total stranger to him less than twelve hours ago.

Within a day her whole world had changed. Yesterday there were two people in the car. Today there were three. Alik strapped the baby in the back, then drove them into town as if they were a normal husband and wife out for a ride with the family.

She didn't understand when he pulled up in front of a car dealership. After darting him a questioning glance he said, "We can't very well drive around in my truck. Let's take a look at a four-door station wagon. They're a good, safe car for children."

How he knew that information, she wasn't sure. She didn't own a car, but was given the use of one of her parents' cars when she needed it. In any event, the car he had in mind would never have been in her price range.

But in agreeing to the terms of his bargain, she'd placed herself in his hands. He was the one who would be making the decisions for the next month. With Alik taking care of them, they would never want for anything.

A half hour later they left to do the shopping for

Nicky. By the time they'd made their purchases, which would include the latest safety infant seat, their new car would be ready to drive home.

Now that he was a father, shopping with Alik was like having her own personal Santa Claus.

"No more!" she cried when he added a music box mobile of the Winnie the Pooh characters to their carts. "We'll never fit everything inside the trailer as it is. In fact I'm not sure the rental car isn't going to drag on the ground with all these purchases."

"We'll pick up the new one before we go grocery shopping."

Close to noon they were ready to head back to the site. The rental had been returned. Alik got into his truck. Blaire followed in the sleek black station wagon, which was jammed full of more stuff than any little boy would ever need.

After those busy hours, all he wanted was another bottle and a nap. Blaire tried to hide her amusement because the second they'd pulled up to the back of the trailer, Alik had discovered the range of his son's considerable lung power.

As he extricated the baby from the new infant seat, he flashed her an anxious look. She grabbed the diaper bag and followed them into the trailer. Nicky's howling could probably be heard for miles.

Of necessity Alik had to use his shoe to clear a trail through his books and charts so she could find a place to sit on the couch. He handed her the baby.

"You stay there with him while I fix another bottle of the canned formula. Later you can show me how to make the other kind."

Thirty seconds later he returned from the sink and plunged the nipple into Nicky's mouth without showing any sign of hesitation as he'd done last night. Alik was a fast learner.

"I'll start bringing in the things from the car," he muttered, but his gaze stayed riveted on their noisy son who drank his milk with the same relish Alik had devoured his breakfast. He was an adorable child.

Blaire kept her head down, trying not to smile. In fact she was so happy, she was afraid this was a dream and she might wake up. To be with Alik again, to know she and Nicky were going to be living with him for the next month, filled her with inexpressible joy.

She refused to think about the day they would have to leave Alik and fly back to California, bringing an end to this blissful state. Then her hell would begin because she would only be allowed to see him when it was his turn for visitation.

Make the most of it now, Blaire, because this is all you'll ever get.

While Alik was outside, his cell phone rang. Though she was tempted to answer in case it was something important, she didn't dare. It might be one of his parents or his married brother or sister. Under no circumstances could they know she was back in New York, or worse, find out she and the baby were staying with Alik.

Blaire put the baby against her shoulder to burp him and waited to talk to Alik until he'd come in with the last load of boxes. The living room of the trailer looked like a small warehouse stacked to the ceiling.

"Alik? You had a phone call a minute ago, but I didn't answer it because I don't want anyone to know I'm here."

A frown marred his sun-bronzed features. "Rick

already knows,'' he snarled, ''so what difference does it make.''

''I—I was referring to your family. After what I did to you, I know they have a horrible opinion of me.'' *I have the battle scars to prove it.* ''Since this arrangement is temporary, I would prefer we kept it private.'' She lifted her head to look up at him with gray eyes full of pleading. ''Is that too much to ask?''

A tiny pulse hammered along the side of his strong jaw. His narrowed gaze raked her face and hair. She couldn't tell what he was thinking.

''I have voice mail, so don't worry about it.''

''Thank you,'' she whispered.

His chest heaved. ''The first act of business is to set up the crib. I'll put it in the bedroom where you're going to sleep.''

''No, Alik. I'm not going to take your bed. I can sleep here on the couch. When I have to get up to fix his bottles, the kitchen's just a few steps away.''

He stood there without reacting. ''I want you in the back. My work has me coming and going at odd hours. There's no point in disturbing Nicky's sleep unnecessarily.''

''But this couch isn't big enough or strong enough for you.''

''I'll survive. In South America I slept in a canvas hammock. The couch is divine by comparison. Besides, I have an air mattress, which will cover a multitude of sins.''

So saying, he found the crib box and pushed it along the floor of the trailer into the bedroom. She heard several unintelligible epithets as he bumped into doorways and paraphernalia en route. When the cell phone rang again, he asked her to look at the caller ID and tell him who it was.

With all the noise going on, she thought Nicky might still be awake after his bottle. But the shopping spree must have worn him out. He was dead to the world. She reached for the phone lying next to the diaper bag.

"There's no name, but it's a 307 area code."

"Will you answer it and relay the message?"

Blaire had no desire to speak to anyone, but she couldn't ignore his request. She pressed the Talk button. "Dr. Jarman's residence."

A deep male voice said hello. After a slight hesitation he asked for Alik.

"May I tell him who's calling?"

"It's Dominic." The barest trace of French accent came through.

She couldn't prevent the slight gasp that escaped. "You're a man!"

His low chuckle sounded a lot like Alik's. "Last time I checked I was. I feel like one."

"I—I'm sorry," she stammered, horribly embarrassed. "I thought you were a—"

"Woman?" he answered for her in a teasing voice. "My name's spelled with a *C* on the end. The feminine version ends in *que*."

"Of course. Please forgive me." *Oh, Blaire. You fool!*

"There's no harm done."

She turned her head toward the front door. "D-don't tell Alik," she whispered guiltily.

"Don't tell me what?" Alik called from the kitchen area.

She jerked around to face him. "It's n-nothing. Really!"

He studied her until she stirred restlessly on the couch. "I've almost finished setting up the crib. Ask Dom to give me twenty minutes and I'll phone him back."

She put the phone to her ear once more. "Dominic?"

"I heard him, and will expect his call. Thank you for being such a charming go-between."

Whoever the man was, Blaire instinctively liked him. "You're welcome. Goodbye."

Needing to channel her energy with something physical, she lay Nicky on the couch and propped the quilt so he couldn't possibly fall. Then she started rummaging in sacks for the crib sheet and pads. Once she'd found them, she joined Alik who'd just finished assembling the baby bed.

"I'm glad we chose the walnut. It's beautiful, Alik. Thank you for everything. You've been far too generous."

The angry glint in his eyes shocked her. "I'm his father," he muttered coldly. "You don't need to thank me for things that in any normal household would constitute a given."

She moistened her lips nervously. "I didn't mean to upset you. I only wanted you to know how much I appreciate what you've done. Why don't I make up the crib while you phone your friend back. Nicky's out for the count."

He didn't say anything. To her chagrin he waited and watched her undo the packages. She was all thumbs. Finally they were able to put on the sheet.

He helped her fasten the pads, all in a Winnie the Pooh motif.

"I'll get the mobile."

Before she could tell him she would do that, he'd found the box. In a few seconds he'd fastened it to the bed.

"Nicky's going to love it." Her voice quivered with emotions ready to spill all over the place.

"Let's find out, shall we?"

A second time he deserted her. When he returned, he held the baby whose eyes were now open. Blaire had an idea Alik had wakened him on purpose, but she couldn't be angry with him. Not when he was so eager to see how Nicky would react to his new environment.

They both laughed when the baby made a huge yawn and then promptly went right back to sleep.

"This is his sleepy time. He'll be a lot more fun around five. That's when he has his bath. He'll love the new little tub you picked out with the starfish."

Staring down at him he said, "How much do you think he can see?"

"I don't honestly know, but he responds to colors like crazy. This mobile is perfect."

"He responds to everything about *you*." If that was an accusation, then he'd found his mark. "How much time has he spent with your fiancé?"

Her eyes closed tightly. The lie about Rick was having greater and greater ramifications.

"H-hardly any since he was born because the doctor wanted the baby to get the best start possible. He told me to keep him away from people as much as possible until his six-week checkup. The few times

Rick and I have gone out, mom and dad have tended Nicky. I haven't wanted him to be with anyone else.''

Though Alik didn't say anything, her comment seemed to have appeased him somewhat.

''I've got several students to check up on at the site, but I should be back within an hour. You might as well take a nap while I'm gone. When I return we'll have lunch and get busy organizing the rest of the trailer.''

Without waiting for a response from her, he headed for the living room. She watched him reach for his cell phone before he disappeared out the door.

Blaire took a deep breath and surveyed her kingdom. It was in total chaos, but she didn't care. Alik would be coming back to them in a little while. That was all that mattered.

His suggestion that she lie down made the most sense. Since her arrival in Warwick, so much had happened; she felt she'd lived several lifetimes. Emotionally and physically drained, she started walking to the bedroom, but a rap on the door caused her to turn around.

Before she could reach it to find out who was on the other side, someone pushed it open. ''Dr. Jarman?'' a female voice inquired.

Bristling from the woman's unauthorized entry, Blaire opened the door a little wider to confront the good-looking blond interloper, never mind that Blaire herself had done the exact same thing yesterday. The young woman staring boldly at her out of icy blue eyes had to be close in age to Blaire's twenty-three years.

''Dr. Jarman's out at the site. May I help you?''

''Who are you?''

How long had this been going on?

Ignoring her question Blaire said, "His consultation time is from four to five if you want to make an appointment."

"No, thanks. This is personal."

Blaire decided to take a calculated risk. "Did he ask you to come in and wait for him?"

A red stain appeared on her cheeks. "No. But we're all a pretty casual bunch. If you'd been around here for a while, you would know that."

It was on the tip of Blaire's tongue to ask if Dr. Jarman made a habit of entering her trailer uninvited. But she wisely refrained. Until she had a talk with Alik later in the day, she didn't know what he wanted the people at the site to think about their situation.

Blaire knew what she'd like to tell this hormone-filled, self-proclaimed goddess, but she managed to restrain herself. Barely.

"I'm sure if you walk around, you'll find him."

"I'm sure I will."

Not wanting to appear rude, Blaire waited until the obnoxious student sauntered off before she shut the door. She would have loved to slam it. The only thing that stopped her was Nicky. Blaire needed him to stay asleep so she could have a nap, too.

On Alik's bed.

It took a lot to shock Dominic Giraud, Alik's colleague and one of his best friends who lived in Wyoming. But shock was the only emotion Alik could hear in the other man's voice.

Alik's other good friend, Zane Broderick, who lived in Tooele, Utah, still had to be told. The mammoth project the three of them were working on required their total concentration. But Blaire's arrival with Nicky had caused every other consideration to flee his mind.

"That was your *ex-fiancée* on the phone?"

"The one and only."

"She broke up with you knowing she was pregnant with your child?" he demanded angrily. Alik could always depend on Dom for support.

He heaved a tortured sigh. "She said she didn't discover her condition until after the deed was done. And naturally after that she felt she shouldn't say anything because it would just cause more suffering, so—"

"*Mon Dieu,*" he broke in savagely. Alik knew what Dom was thinking. It was the same thing Alik had been thinking. But hearing Dom's reaction caused him to live the pain all over again.

After a long pause, "You have a son!"

"I do."

"There's no doubt in your mind he's yours?"

Alik swallowed hard. "One glance at him and you would know the answer to that question."

"Your mirror image, *mon vieux?*" Dom often referred to Alik as "old man." It was a French term of endearment he used with Zane as well.

"Blaire's in there somewhere, too."

"Of course."

"Hell, Dom. This has knocked me sideways."

"You're a lucky man to have a son," he muttered deep in his throat. "Whatever else Blaire has done to you, at least she had the decency to inform you. Some women I've known—"

"Say no more."

"Does she want to get back together?"

Alik was biting down so hard, he ground his teeth together. "No. She's getting married in two months. After telling me I was too old for her, she's probably found a hormone-charged kid her own age who doesn't have a dime to his name. My guess is she's hoping for enough child support to keep her and her intended in a lavish lifestyle."

"Is she still sticking to the story that she's too young for you?" The compassion was self-evident in Dom's voice.

"Yes."

There was a significant pause. "You want to know what I think?"

"Go ahead. I need to hear a voice of sanity. I'm afraid all rational thought went out the window when I found her in my trailer." *Looking more gorgeous than ever.*

"I don't buy her reason for breaking up with you. I never did. Now that she has presented you with your son, I'm convinced of it. Alik— If she'd truly fallen out of love with you, she wouldn't have gone near you or the site, certainly not with your son in tow. There's something else going on here."

"Unless she's more mercenary than I thought!" Alik bit out the words. "It's possible that despite her hatred of me, she's making damn sure he gets the inheritance to which he's entitled. If that's the case, then she never knew me at all. You know how I feel about that after everything that has gone on in my family." Dom understood a great deal about Alik's past.

"I do."

"She came as Lady Bountiful, graciously allowing me to bask in her presence. She even let me know I could visit my son once in a while, but I shouldn't forget that Rick Hammond would be the man raising Nicky, calling him son.''

Dom said another French word Alik didn't need to have translated to understand.

''When she'd finished the pretty little speech she'd obviously been practicing on for weeks, I told her the only way there would be visitation was if she lived with me for the next month so I could get to know my son.''

''That must have knocked the foundations from under her.''

''Oh, it did. Believe me.''

''Did she agree?''

''I didn't give her a choice. It was either that, or I told her I would sue for full custody of Nicky and she would never see him again. That's when she caved in.''

Alik could hear his friend's brilliant mind turning everything over. ''Thirty days should give you long enough to discover why she ended your engagement.''

''That reason doesn't matter anymore.''

''If you say so, *mon ami*.'' Dom had always maintained there were other reasons for the sudden breakup.

Alik had always thought so as well, but recently he'd come to the conclusion that it was wishful thinking on his part. He was in a fight for survival. If he let Blaire get to him now, he'd never be free of her power over him.

''The important thing here is Nicky. I plan to be the only father in his life. I'll pay support, but I intend to take a fully active role in rearing him. There will be no inheritance. One day when that sinks in, she's going to regret the impulse to walk into my life uninvited with our offspring.''

He cleared his throat. "The more I think about it, the more I'm convinced she was never on the pill. I slept with her before we were married because she begged me to. We made love for the obvious reasons, but deep down I sensed an insecurity in her that led me to believe she needed that intimacy before I left for that seminar.

"Hell, Dom. I got trapped in the oldest game known to man and didn't even see it coming!"

"Maybe. Maybe not."

"It all fits!" Alik growled.

"You mean the way it all fit when I *thought* I'd been taken for the same ride? Do you remember the night before my wedding when you and Zane came aboard the yacht in Nice and found me in the same shape you're in now?"

Alik blinked. "That's not something I'm likely to forget."

"Nor I. I almost lost Hannah because of it."

"My situation's not the same at all."

"It never is when a man is in the kind of pain you're in. But I heard something a little while ago you didn't."

He gripped the phone a little tighter. "What are you talking about?"

"Let me ask you a question. What does Blaire know about me?"

"Nothing. You and I became friends after she broke our engagement."

"So you've never mentioned my name?"

"As a matter of fact, it did come up in the conversation this morning. Why?"

"When I was on the phone with her and introduced myself, she'd been under the impression that I was a woman."

Alik could remember the exact moment when she'd turned away from him to speak in hushed tones to Dom. "That's not so unusual."

"I agree, except in this case she sounded incredibly relieved... Chew on that for a while. I'll talk to you in a few days when there's been enough time for some of the haze to clear. I predict you'll see a lot better after it does.

"When you get the time, scan a picture of your son on the printer and e-mail it to us. Hannah's going to be overjoyed. In a year's time, Elizabeth and Nicky ought to be so familiar with each other, they'll become lifetime friends.

"A bientôt, mon camarade."

CHAPTER FOUR

"Dr. Jarman? Could I talk to you for a minute?"

Because of the time he'd spent at the site with some students, plus his conversation with Dominic, he'd been gone longer than he'd planned. Almost two hours. He needed to get back to the trailer, and kept on walking.

"I'm afraid I don't have the time right now, Sandy. In fact I'm not going to be available for appointments until the middle of next week."

She had to run to keep up with him. "This isn't about the archaeological dig. I overheard Dr. Fawson say that he was going to hire a secretary to help do some of the paperwork both you and he don't have time for. I volunteered to do the job in the evenings, so he told me to drop by and see if you wanted to share a secretary."

Thank you very much, Dr. Fawson.

He paused midstride. "I appreciate the offer, Sandy, but I already have someone who helps me," he lied.

In reality he'd never wanted a secretary because he'd always worked in the field. The only time he'd been given one was when he'd accepted the position of guest lecturer in San Diego. As for seminars, he only did them on occasion a favor for an old colleague. The last one had been a four-day confab in Kentucky where he'd ended up paying the ultimate price for his absence from Blaire.

Sandy stiffened. "You mean the woman I just spoke to in your trailer?"

Good grief.

"Does she know anything about archaeology or geology?"

Leaning on the inspiration of the moment he said in a smooth tone, "She satisfies my needs nicely. But please thank Dr. Fawson for thinking of me."

To his relief both Nicky and Blaire were still asleep when he entered the bedroom of the trailer a few minutes later. Without being aware of the passage of time, he stood in the doorway to watch them.

Nicky lay in his usual position on his back, his arms outstretched, his hands in tiny fists, his handsome face flawlessly perfect.

Blaire had turned on her side toward the baby, her long flowing hair fanning the pillow like a princess. His Rapunzel with the gleaming chestnut mane. His gaze studied her classical features, then moved downward to the exquisite mold of her body.

The birth of the baby had made her more voluptuous than ever. Five feet six inches of breathtaking flesh and blood. Her jeans revealed the outline of long, slender legs he could feel intertwined with his whenever he allowed himself to remember their night of rapture.

At first she'd been shy and adorable. He'd just held her until her crystalline gray eyes lifted to his with such love and trust in their invitation, he was lost. Her response was more than he'd ever dreamed. Their passion drove them to make love over and over again.

Tears glazed his eyes remembering the beauty of it. His gaze darted to his son. That was the night Nicky was conceived.

Had it all been a role she was playing for his money? If so, she was a superb actress. During those hours of euphoria, she'd had him convinced he was her heart and soul. Her life!

His eyes closed as the blackness of the last year enveloped him.

On the phone Dom had warned him things might not be exactly as they appeared. Blaire *had* returned to the scene of the crime with their baby. Unusual under the circumstances.

You need a few days for the haze to clear.

Obviously in Dom's case, everything had come out right in the end. Alik was thrilled for him and Hannah.

But Blaire wasn't Hannah. His hands bunched into fists. All this time Blaire had kept the knowledge of his son from him.

She's after your money, Jarman.

There was no other explanation.

His eyes looked down at her once more. *At the end of the thirty days, you're in for a shocking surprise, my treacherous love.*

Blaire had been on the verge of waking up when she sensed Alik's presence in the doorway. She opened her eyes in time to see the back of his head before it disappeared.

She wondered how long he'd been standing there. No doubt he'd been checking on Nicky who was still asleep. He ought to be making sounds anytime now, letting them know he wanted to eat and play.

She could hear the clank of metal coming from the kitchen. Feeling guilty because she hadn't prepared lunch, she made up her mind that this would be the last time he came home to find her sacked out on the bed.

Evidently she'd needed the rest more than she'd realized.

Before Nicky demanded their full attention, now might be the best time to talk to Alik about his female visitor. Blaire would just as soon keep her own identity a secret. She imagined he felt the same way. It would be better to know right from the first what he wanted her to say to his students and colleagues.

Alik had always been a private person. There were still things about his past he'd never confided to her because they were too painful. Though he'd become an angry, bitter man since their parting, she didn't think his sense of privacy had changed. In fact she imagined he'd closed up altogether.

Another sin he could add to the list condemning her. Blaire's body trembled. *It was a list she could never defend.*

After slipping on her flats, she went in search of him. The mouthwatering aroma of hot clam chowder and garlic bread filled the interior of the trailer.

He loved seafood. Throughout their courtship, he'd always ordered salmon or scallops or lobster when they'd had dinner at the waterfront.

"Everything's ready. Sit down."

Gone was the tenderness, the little niceties which had made up part of his overwhelming male charm.

It's all your fault, Blaire.

"Thank you. This looks delicious." He'd removed the large map from the table she'd seen the day before. She, in turn, had to clear some things off the chrome chair to sit down. On top of the pile was a poster done in a Western motif. It had to be something Alik had recently acquired.

"My good man, could you tell me where your boss is?" The Wyoming cowboy glared back at the Easterner, spit out his tobacco and said, *"The son of a bitch ain't been born yet!"*

She laughed before she could prevent it. "Where did this come from?"

Alik flashed it a glance before taking his place on the other chair.

"An old Pony Express way station in Laramie. I meant to put it up on the wall, but haven't found the time to get around to it."

"You've been in Wyoming?"

"That's right."

He ate his chowder without comment. Realizing he wouldn't tolerate any chitchat, she thought she'd better ask him the question that had been on her mind since the other woman's visit.

"A student came to see you a little while ago. She just walked in. I asked her if she had an appointment, but it was obvious she didn't. I had no idea what to say. S-she—"

"That was Sandy. I've already talked to her. She assumes you're my new secretary. I think we'll leave it at that."

"But when I don't leave the trailer at night, then—"

"Then everyone can damn well put their own interpretation on it. They will anyway as soon as they get a look at our son."

She shuddered from the iciness in his tone. "I can handle that, but I'd rather no one knew my real name."

A deep frown knit his dark brows together. He flashed her a piercing green regard. "Why in the hell not?"

She had to think fast. "Because everyone's going to think I'm a loose woman. There'll be talk. If may not be important to you, but I don't want to besmirch my parents' good name."

He finished off a second piece of garlic bread. "Then call yourself Ms. Hammond."

Blaire grabbed at the lifeline he'd thrown her without his realizing it. "Thank you for being so understanding." *Thank you, Alik. Now your family won't find out I'm here.*

"It makes no difference to me. It's going to be your lawful name in a couple of months anyway. Since we anticipated our wedding vows with Nicky the result, I don't imagine your fiancé will mind if you take on his name before you tie yourselves to each other," he lashed out, even though he'd maintained a quiet voice.

"Speaking of our son, do you have some recent snaps of him?"

"Yes! Dozens of them at every stage of his development so far."

"Good. Dominic wants to see what he looks like."

After another spoonful of soup she said, "He sounded very nice on the phone. How did you meet him?"

Alik's enigmatic gaze played over her face. "It's a long story. Zane will want pictures, too."

"Another good friend?" she ventured, then could have bitten her tongue out for sounding too curious. But he could have no idea how much she was dying inside for every little crumb he was willing to throw in her direction that would tell her about his life since she'd run away from him.

"Yes."

His clipped answer revealed she'd been treading on sacred ground. Afraid to sit this close to him for fear she might burst from the love she felt for him, she got up from the table and cleared it.

"While I do the dishes and make his formula, why don't you find Nicky's new tub. By the time it's filled, he'll be awake and ready for his bath."

Despite his animosity toward her, she derived great comfort in knowing the three of them were together under the same roof. From the second the doctor had told her she was pregnant, she'd dreamed about domestic scenes like this every night since.

She'd hugged other dreams to herself as well. Those moments of shared intimacy. The passion. But circumstances beyond her control had brought that joy to a crashing halt.

Now, unbelievably, she was in his life again, but only as the mother of his child. A temporary reprieve until he felt comfortable enough to be alone with his son.

You may look, but you may not touch. You may love, but only in secret.

"Tears so soon?" He plopped the tub on the counter she'd finished wiping off. "I agree it's hell being away from the one you love. May I remind you that this was your decision, not mine."

Alik's cruel mockery, delivered with such excruciating accuracy, was something she would never get used to. But at least he thought she was missing her fiancé. So far her ruse had protected her. The trick was to keep it up for the entire month of October.

"Oh— I can hear Nicky."

"I'll get him."

The next half hour proved to be sheer delight. Alik lowered the baby into the water and bathed him per Blaire's instructions. His little chin quivered as his daddy washed his hair with the glycerin soap. But after that, his excitement became so intense, he couldn't stop moving his arms and legs at the same time. The cherubic smile on his face would have melted anyone's heart. Already she could tell he was the light of his daddy's eye.

Laughter rumbled out of Alik. It thrilled her to the very core of her being. By the time he'd lifted Nicky onto the towel, the front of his polo shirt was sopping wet. But she knew he wasn't cognizant of anything except the pure joy of taking care of his son.

He watched her use a Q-tip to clean one ear, then he took over to do the other. While he finished with the powder and diapered him, Blaire had a warm bottle ready. Soon Nicky was clean as a pin and dressed in a white stretchy suit with little lambs on the collar, providing the perfect foil for all his black curls.

Alik took the formula from her and carried Nicky over to the couch. He no longer treated him like he was about to break. His actions were entirely natural as he propped him in his arm and started to feed him.

It gave her an idea. She started looking for her overnight bag among the boxes and sacks.

"What are you doing?"

"I want my Polaroid camera. There's still some film in it. As long as your friends would like pictures, they should have at least one showing the proud papa holding his son."

The fact that he didn't tell her not to bother meant

the idea pleased him. When she found what she was looking for, she used up the rest of the film taking shots at various angles. These particular pictures were precious. She would guard them with her life. But for the time being, she put them on the couch next to him.

"Alik?" He lifted his head in the middle of examining one of them. "I-is it all right if I take a shower now?"

His veiled eyes swept over her, bringing the heat to her cheeks. "Of course. It's probably the best idea. This trailer doesn't have a big water tank. I'll plan to shower at night before I turn in. As long as we stagger the times, there should always be enough hot water for the three of us."

The three of us. What divine words.

An hour later she walked in the living room dressed in a pair of jeans and another sweater, her freshly shampooed hair blow-dried and caught at the nape with a ribbon.

No one was there. She'd been deserted.

Nicky's bottle stood on the counter. He'd drained every drop. The empty stroller box had been left on the kitchen floor. It was the kind that worked like an infant seat until the baby could sit up on his own. On the table were the contents of the diaper bag where she always kept his zipper suit to wear outside.

Undoubtedly Alik was so enamored of Nicky, he wanted to show him off to everyone. The mess could wait.

With an ache in her heart and a smile on her lips, she started to straighten the front room. It truly was a disaster. She made five trips outside to rid the trailer of the empty cartons. The only thing to do was place them along the side for Alik to deal with.

Just putting her's and the baby's personal things away in the bedroom along with their luggage, was a monumental task.

Finally she could get down to the real problem. Alik's paraphernalia.

What amazed her were the number of notebooks and geological journals he'd accumulated. Crammed between papers and reference materials associated with his work was his computer. She also spied a scanning electron microscope, plus a TV tray with a hand lens and rock hammer.

Since he had to have a place to sleep, she needed to make some kind of order out of the chaos.

It was a good thing she'd decided to put on sandals. Over in the corner on the floor she found a broken scotch bottle, shattered glass and a damaged microscope.

"Leave that, Blaire. I'll clean it up."

She gasped and whirled around. "I didn't hear you come in."

"I should have knocked. I apologize. I guess I'm not used to anyone else being here when I walk in."

"Naturally not."

"From now on I'll lock the door as I leave, and knock before I use a key to get back in. If you do the same, we won't have a problem. I have another key around here someplace. I'll find it and give it to you later."

"That's fine." Her gaze strayed from his arresting face to Nicky's. "Did the two of you enjoy your walk?"

He kissed the baby's head. "Very much. Nicky has just had his first lesson in geology."

"How did the stroller work out?"

"Not that well in the dirt. I decided to stow it in the back of the station wagon. In town it will be a necessity. Around here I'll stick to carrying him."

"D-did you meet anyone?"

His eyes followed the motion of her hands as she rubbed her hips nervously.

"Just about everybody who lives at the site," he answered suavely. "They knew he was my son the second they laid eyes on him. Nicky was a real hit. He didn't cry once.

"Dr. Fawson, the resident archaeologist, has five daughters and told me I was a lucky devil, which of course I am.

"All the female students clamored to hold him. I told them he was still too young to be passed around. They needed to give him a little more time to become accustomed to his new surroundings.

"We came back because he started looking around for you. Why don't you take him while I set up the playpen. Then he can lie there and watch me while I work at the table."

She reached for the baby and cuddled him close. He smelled of powder and the soap Alik used in the shower.

His rounded cheeks felt cool from being in the early-evening air. "Come on, sweetheart. Let's get you out of this suit while your daddy makes more messes.

"Honestly, Alik." She put the baby on the couch to take off his coverall. "I don't know how we'll move around here if you set it up."

"We'll manage." He leaned over to kiss him once more. "You want to be by your father, don't you, little guy."

Blaire trembled inside because it was patently clear Alik had fallen in love with Nicky. It was the forever kind of love. By bringing the baby to New York, she'd set a force in motion that had taken on a life of its own. She could either ride the crest, or face losing her son.

Of course she'd already made her choice, but it meant her life had been irrevocably changed. Though she would grow old alone, Alik would always be on the fringe of it because of Nicky.

He was their son, their common bond. Through him, she would never cease to watch for Alik, to wait to hear about him, to wonder what he was doing. Forever and always, she would love him.

"The phone's ringing, Blaire. Would you get it?"

Jerked from her reverie, she picked up Nicky and moved over to the counter.

"This time it's an 801 area code," she informed him.

He was down on the floor reading directions with the playpen half out of the box.

"That'll be Zane. Tell him to hold on."

Blaire did his bidding. Another vibrant male voice was on the other end of the line.

"Am I speaking to Blaire?"

"Yes."

"I understand congratulations are in order. Dom called me a little while ago with the news. I want pictures, too!"

She smiled. "I took some tonight with Alik holding the baby."

"That's a sight I've got to see."

Oh, Alik. Your friends are wonderful. I wish I knew them. What I'd give to be your wife, to live the rest of my life with you.

"If you'll be patient for a minute longer, Alik will talk to you. Right now he's erecting a playpen."

A burst of laughter resounded in her ears. "A new little chip off the old block. I think I'm going to have to make a trip out to New York right away."

"Where do you live?"

"For the time being, Tooele, Utah."

"That's near the Great Salt Lake, isn't it?"

"Yes. I see you know your geography."

She smiled. "Have you been swimming in it? Do you really float like a cork?"

He laughed again. "Absolutely! You'll have to try it sometime."

"I've always wanted t—"

"Mind if I cut in?" Alik muttered behind her. She felt the warmth of his breath against the side of her neck, but the hint of menace in his tone led her to believe he didn't like her chatting with his friend.

"Just a minute, Zane. Here's Alik," she said in a shaky voice, then handed him the phone.

Thank heaven for the baby she could clutch to her heart at anytime and receive unqualified love. Leaving Alik to his privacy, she went into the bedroom and changed his diaper.

This was his favorite time of evening. She wound up the music box. When the tinkling melody filled the room, the mobile turned around on its own. Nicky watched the movement of the various colored characters as if mesmerized. She could tell he was stimulated because his arms and legs kicked in constant motion.

It didn't take Alik long to come looking for his son, but when he saw Nicky's response to the mobile, he stood by the crib to watch in fascination. Blaire couldn't handle being next to him.

"I'm going to start dinner, Alik. You bought enough groceries for a week. Is there anything particular you're craving tonight?"

"Since you asked, how about some of your shrimp tacos?"

Those were her favorites, too. She'd fixed them for him several times at the house, but hadn't made them again since their breakup.

"Blaire—"

Suddenly there was tension. She stopped at the doorway. "Yes?"

"If you want to talk to your fiancé, go ahead. I'll stay in here with Nicky for a while."

Her breath caught. "Thank you."

"Shut the door behind you."

This was the part of the lie she hated most.

Because she needed to vent her feelings, she found the keys to the new car and took the cell phone outside with her. Aunt Diana, her mother's younger sister, had been the one to lend her the diamond ring. She was more than a relative. She was a true friend and confidante. Right now she was the person Blaire wanted to talk to.

Except that the second she heard her aunt's voice, she broke down sobbing and couldn't stop. Ten minutes must have gone by before she apologized to her aunt and told her she would phone the next day when she'd had some sleep.

After wiping her eyes, Blaire went back inside the trailer. Alik was already scanning pictures on the printer to send to his buddies. Nicky lay in the playpen staring up at his father. The scene was so sweet, Blaire could have shed another bucket of tears.

Instead she hurried through to the kitchen to start dinner. Once or twice she felt Alik's searching gaze, but he never said anything. She knew her face was splotchy from crying. In his mind it provided more evidence that she was missing the man she was going to marry.

Alik finally spoke once they sat down at the table to eat. "I take it you informed your fiancé of the situation."

She nodded.

"If you find you can't live without him, you're free to fly out to see him for a visit, as long as you leave Nicky with me."

Blaire couldn't look at him. "No. We made a bargain and I'll stick to it."

"Even if it kills you."

His goading caught her on the raw. "What more do you want from me?" she cried out in frustration.

"So help me, more than you were ever capable of giving." His voice sounded haunted. In the next instant he stood up, but his chair accidentally screeched against the floor. Nicky burst into frightened tears.

They both reached for him, but Alik got there first. Almost immediately the baby quieted down. Already he felt safe in his father's arms.

"You look exhausted, Blaire. Why don't you go to bed. I'll clean up in here and give Nicky a bottle before I put him down. I plan to get up with him at three as well."

"You don't have to do that."

"I want to. For the next while I think it's important he be with me during the nights. Then we can start taking turns."

Maybe it was for the best. With their emotions so near the surface, the raw tension had caused both of them to erupt. She couldn't afford to let it happen again.

"Before I say good night, would you mind telling me what time you want breakfast?"

"Why don't we discuss everything tomorrow. I'm taking a few days off to give Nicky my exclusive attention. There'll be plenty of time to talk about a routine then."

She averted her eyes. "All right."

Much as she wanted to rise up on tiptoe and kiss Nicky, she didn't dare. His face was too close to Alik's.

As she turned to leave, he gripped her upper arm with his free hand. "How old is your fiancé?"

Please. No more.

"Why do you want to know?" She tried to ease out of his grasp, but he held her fast.

"You can say that after telling me I was too old for you?" he said scathingly. Only now was she beginning to understand the depth of his hurt. "I'm asking because I want to know the kind of man my son is going to be around."

She could hardly breathe. "He's twenty-four."

"What does he do for a living?"

"He works construction."

"Has he been to college?"

"He went to a junior college for two years."

"Have you been to bed with him?"

Flame scorched her cheeks. "That's none of your business."

"Just in case you're pregnant again, I happen to think it's very relevant since I only plan to pay child support for my own child, not his."

She twisted away from him, almost incapacitated by pain. *His pain.* "I'm going to forget you said that."

He followed her into the bedroom. "You're running away again. Does your fiancé even know you and I were engaged? And if he does, have you told him why you broke it off?"

"Rick knows everything! All right?"

There was that whiteness around his mouth again. If they had to live through another night like this, it would destroy them both. She had to do something to stop the pain from escalating.

"Alik—it was never a case of your being too old. I'm the one who had the problem. I felt too young for you, too inexperienced."

It was the truth. In the beginning she'd had a hard time believing someone like Dr. Jarman would ever be interested in one of his students. But all that changed after he drove her home from the university that wonderful day.

"You have an intelligence and sophistication few women could match. I'm just an ordinary girl from San Diego who's never been anywhere or done anything to distinguish myself. I have no particular talent. I'm not like you and never could be.

"The closer it got to our wedding, the more I feared I would hold you back by being your wife. The reason I begged you to make love to me before you went to Kentucky was that I thought that at least in bed, I could be your equal.

"But however much I enjoyed making love with you, I had to face myself the next day. I was still the same ordinary girl in the mirror who could never measure up to you. The last thing I wanted was to be a burden to you, or embarrass you. That's why I ran away.

"With Rick I don't have any of those fears because he's as ordinary as I am. I hope that answers your questions once and for all.

"Good night."

CHAPTER FIVE

"MS. HAMMOND?"

Blaire kept walking in the brisk fall air before she remembered Ms. Hammond was the name she was known by at the site. She halted in her tracks and turned her head in surprise.

The blond, good-looking male graduate student she'd met when she'd first been searching for Alik had just stepped out of his trailer.

She shaded her eyes. "Hello."

His half smile probably charmed every female student on the premises. "Hi. I'm Lane Atwood. This is only the second time I've seen you, and it's been a week already! That baby must keep you busy. I'm surprised he's not with you right now."

"Dr. Jarman took him to town to do errands."

After lunch Alik had decided she'd been too cooped up with Nicky and needed some time off by herself. When they'd gone, the trailer had felt so empty, she'd cleaned the whole place spotless. Anything to fill the time. But it still hung heavy so she decided to go out for exercise. Now she was sorry.

He cocked his head. "The way you address him— does this mean you two aren't an item?" He made little circles in front of his chest with his index fingers to stress his point. "Please don't be offended by my question. Sandy told me you're his nanny-cum-secretary."

I'll just bet she did.

"I'm surprised she didn't mention that I'm wearing an engagement ring."

His expression didn't alter as he caught sight of it. "Dr. Jarman's?"

A fresh pain pierced her heart. "No."

His blue eyes reflected male admiration as they traveled over her body dressed in a suede jacket and jeans. "How soon is the wedding?"

"Seven weeks."

"So where is your fiancé?"

After the flare-up with Alik, she'd hoped she wouldn't have to talk about this subject again.

"In California."

Before the words were out, she regretted satisfying his curiosity about anything to do with her personal life, never mind that they were lies. This is what came of wandering around the site without Alik. She wouldn't do it again.

"You're a long way from home, and probably missing him. Why don't you come to a party at one of the trailers tonight? We listen to a little music, cook up a little ethnic food. Everyone's cool. How about it?"

"I appreciate being included, but I'm afraid I couldn't come. Dr. Jarman does his writing in the evenings. That's when his son is the most demanding. But thank you for asking me."

She started walking again. He caught up to her. "Where are you going so fast?"

"I thought I'd take a look around the site."

"You haven't seen it yet?"

"No. A baby requires twenty-four-hour care."

After getting settled into a routine, Alik had pretty

much ignored her over the last four days. She knew nothing about his work here, and had been afraid to ask for fear he'd bite her head off.

"Well you're free now. Allow me to be your guide."

He was beginning to annoy her. "That's all right. I'm sure you have responsibilities to carry out."

"No, I don't. This is my afternoon off. To be honest, I've looked for you every day hoping to spend some time with you. How much longer will you be taking care of his son?"

She sucked in her breath. "Another three weeks."

"Dr. Jarman has a reputation for being a hard-driving taskmaster, but I doubt he expects you to be on duty every day and night. Surely he won't mind if you get out for a few hours tonight."

Lane had it all wrong. Like everyone else around here, he probably assumed she was sharing Alik's bed. Telling Lane she was engaged hadn't fazed him. No doubt he hoped to ply her with drinks at the party and let come what may.

Under other circumstances Blaire would have loved to let nature take its course, but only with Alik. Little did Lane know *she* was the one who didn't want to be parted from Nicky's father, not even if he ignored her after he came in from work. He'd hurt her terribly when he'd driven the baby into Warwick without her.

The time was flying by. Too soon they wouldn't be a family of three anymore. No matter his brooding demeanor around the trailer when he wasn't playing with his son, she couldn't bear the thought of separation!

"He's given me this afternoon off," she said in her

breeziest manner, hoping he got the point, and headed toward the break in the trees.

In the distance a large area had been cleared of vegetation. At least a dozen students were on their hands and knees with tools inside a pit as big and deep as an Olympic-size swimming pool. "What's going on over there?"

"Dr. Jarman was working on his own project, and discovered this pit. It's full of bones. He contacted Dr. Fawson who has declared this a major archaeological site. What you're looking at is only the tip of the iceberg."

Blaire could see some bones partially buried by dirt the students were unearthing. To work at a dig this important would be a real thrill. "You're saying there's a lot more to uncover?"

"That's right. It will take years."

"How old are the bones?"

He eyed her speculatively. "You and Dr. Jarman must not spend much time talking about his work."

She felt her temper flare. This definitely wasn't a good idea. "Not when there's a newborn around needing constant care."

"Where's the mother?"

Blaire had had enough of his interrogation. "Why do you ask?"

He flashed her a benign smile. "Sandy wants to know who her competition is."

Ah. Sandy. "I suggest that if she is that interested, she should ask Dr. Jarman herself."

"She's tried, but so far she hasn't been able to get to first base."

The news put to rest once and for all any fears Blaire had harbored on that score.

"Then Sandy has her answer and shouldn't send you on a pointless fishing expedition for her."

He shook his head. "Come on. I was asking for myself, too. I don't know how to make it any plainer that I'd like to get to know you better."

Before she went back to the trailer she said, "As I told you a little while ago, I'm in love with my fiancé. I'll go to my grave loving him," her voice shook, "so I don't know how *I* can make it any plainer to you."

"*You heard, Ms. Hammond, Atwood,*" a forbidding, yet familiar male voice interjected behind them.

While Blaire's heart tripped over itself, Lane's face paled. In Alik's presence, the younger man's macho image vanished. She'd never been so happy to see anyone in her life, but she had to school her reaction so she wouldn't give her feelings away.

Avoiding Alik's probing gaze, she reached blindly for Nicky who cuddled right up against her shoulder and chin.

"If I discover you bothering Ms. Hammond again, you're off the project, even if you are Dr. Fawson's bright boy. Do you understand me?"

Blaire actually had the grace to feel sorry for Lane, no matter how brash and foolish he'd been. Anyone who had to deal with Alik under negative circumstances would never come out the winner. His powerful physical demeanor, let alone his intelligence and authoritative aura intimidated young and old alike.

Since she didn't want to hear Lane's answer and feel more embarrassed for him, she began her walk back through the trees toward the trailers. The evening shadows reminded her it would be getting dark soon.

Nicky's face was entirely too kissable. "Daddy must have already given you a bottle. Did you have fun with him in town?"

She quickened her steps to reach home before Alik. Knowing he would subject her to a torturous inquisition of his own, she needed a minute to compose herself before she had to face him.

The second she unlocked the trailer door, the delicious aroma of Greek food wafted past her nostrils. He'd brought them dinner. The sacks were sitting on the counter. No wonder he'd come looking for her!

After putting Nicky down in the playpen with his pacifier, she rushed into the kitchen to set the table and put on some sodas. He'd brought everything she loved. Souvlaki, gyros, green salad, lemon rice.

"This looks wonderful," she said as he entered the trailer with a grim expression on his face. "Let's eat while it's still hot."

"Did he come to the trailer looking for you?" Alik demanded without preamble, not making any sign that he was ready to sit down to his meal.

She took her place at the table anyway. "No. He saw me as I passed his trailer."

"You mean he was lying in wait for you." The words came out more like a hiss.

"In all fairness to him, he was acting like any college guy his age who's still out for a good time wherever he can find it. There was no harm done."

"Maybe I shouldn't have interfered."

Blaire hated that silky voice he used to underline his unsubtle innuendos.

"Actually I'm glad you did. His questions embarrassed me. To be honest, I felt like a fool."

By now his handsome, bronzed face looked like a

thundercloud. With careless grace he caught the leg of the chair with his boot, pulled it out and sat down.

"Go on," he prodded tersely.

She took a deep breath. "Sandy has told everyone I'm your secretary and baby tender. I guess it sounded pretty suspicious when I didn't have the slightest idea about the work you're doing here. He didn't buy the argument that the baby's needs had come before everything else. I'm afraid if anyone else asks questions I can't answer, that excuse won't wash with them, either."

While she bit into a gyro, he lounged back in his chair, staring at her through narrowed lids. So far he hadn't touched his food. The tension between them was so palpable, she could scarcely swallow hers.

"What do you want to know?"

After several gulps of soda she said, "It would help if I knew what brought you to Warwick in the first place, a-and what's so important about this pit you discovered."

Except for the baby noises coming from the playpen, another minute of excruciating silence went by.

"After dinner I'll show you." On that note he tucked in to the souvlaki.

Relieved to hear his grudging rejoinder, she ate the rest of her meal before getting up to make coffee. He always enjoyed a cup with his dessert.

Tonight he could finish off the rest of the apple pie she'd baked for him yesterday. When the baby napped, there wasn't anything else to do but cook and read. He didn't have a TV, not that she minded.

When they'd started dating, they'd both agreed that they wouldn't have a TV in their home once they were married. There were still newspapers and the radio.

Her eyes closed as she remembered Alik whispering against her lips, "We probably won't even make it around to those since I plan on being otherwise occupied with my gorgeous wife for the rest of my nights."

"If you can get your mind off your fiancé long enough to wipe the table, I'll get my map."

Her eyes flew open. This was one time when she had no easy comeback. Hoping he couldn't see her flushed face, she scrubbed the top with a dishcloth. She would have gotten a bottle warmed for Nicky, but he didn't need one yet.

Out of the corner of her eye she watched Alik return from the area next to his computer carrying something large rolled up with an elastic band. When he undid it, she let out a small cry of recognition.

Ever alert, Alik's keen gaze played over her features. "What's wrong?"

"Nothing. It's just that I remember seeing it on the table when I came into the trailer to wait for you that first morning. I—I've wondered about it ever since."

He smoothed it out on the flat surface.

After talking to his friends, the names of Tooele and Laramie had a little more meaning for Blaire. By tacit agreement they both sat down once more.

"Before you disappeared from my life, I received an invitation to attend a seminar in London having to do with the building of the tunnel under the English Channel.

"At the time, I was under the impression we were going to be married and would be on our honeymoon, so of course I declined. But as I found out in

Kentucky, life has a way of happening to you when you had other plans.''

The bitterness in his deep voice made her guilt all the more agonizing.

She heard a sharp intake of breath. ''When I could find no trace of you, I left for England. That's where I met Dominic Giraud and Zane Broderick who were also in attendance. Zane's an engineer. Dom is the man with the vision and the contacts.''

''The vision for what?'' After worrying and wondering about Alik every second since that ghastly time, she hung on any bit of information he was willing to give her.

''In case you and I end up sharing custody, I suppose you're entitled to know that the guys and I are building a bullet train that is going to stretch from Warwick to San Francisco.''

A bullet train?

''Magnetic levitation...'' she murmured. ''I remember learning about that in one of my physics classes. How utterly fantastic!''

''It will be when it's finished.''

His avowal left her in no doubt.

''Our country badly needs transportation like this!'' she cried with enthusiasm. ''So many people would rather see the land as they travel, but they don't want to have to drive or worry about accidents.''

She had the impression he was about to say something more, then thought the better of it.

''How fast will it go?''

''Zane's prototype is hitting over four hundred miles an hour now.''

Blaire shook her head. ''That's incredible! This has

to be the most thrilling project you could ever undertake.''

''You're right.''

His bland reply didn't fool her for a minute. A project like this would have captured his imagination like nothing else. At least God had answered one of her prayers.

She'd asked that He help Alik get on with his life, and could be thankful for that blessing. As for Nicky, she knew he'd already brought the greatest joy possible to his father's life.

Trying to rein in her emotions, she got up to check on the baby. He was such a perfect angel lying there watching and listening to them. The pacifier had fallen out of his mouth, but he didn't seem to mind. She knelt at the side of the webbing and put it back in.

''H-how far having you gotten in procuring rights to the land?'' she stammered.

''Dom is working the Utah/Nevada territory right now.''

''What are those different colors you have marked on the line?''

''They represent the various kinds of soil we'll have to work with to lay track.''

''I see.'' Now everything was making sense. ''What about that huge pit out there?''

''We started to break ground here last month. Suddenly all worked stopped because the bulldozer had uncovered some bones.''

She got to her feet, still looking down at Nicky. ''How old do you estimate the bones in this particular pit?''

"Maybe 400 A.D. They're all over New York State."

A loud enough gasp escaped Blaire's throat to frighten Nicky. "I'm sorry, sweetheart." She bent over to pick him up and cuddle him.

Rocking him back and forth she said, "Lane told me Dr. Fawson had only uncovered a fraction of it."

Suddenly Alik was on his feet. "You mean Atwood actually talked about something else besides trying to get you into bed tonight?"

If she didn't know better, she would think Alik's jealousy had been aroused. But that couldn't possibly be, not when he hated her for what she'd done. She couldn't conceive of the day when he would forgive her.

In an economy of movement he rolled up the map. That signaled the end of their discussion. It would have to last her until she flew to San Diego with Nicky in three weeks' time.

She was planning on that happening because she hadn't broken any part of her bargain with Alik, and didn't intend to.

"He's in love with himself, and isn't that different from a lot of guys his age."

The tiny nerve she'd seen at other times when his emotions were aroused was ticking along his hard jaw. His green eyes turned to flint as they penetrated hers in accusation. "He's the same age as Rick."

Her mouth went dry. *Think quick, Blaire.* "He met me when I was already pregnant. That made our situation entirely different from the beginning."

Without hesitation she put Nicky in his arms. "If you'll change him, I'm going to warm his bottle."

But he didn't leave the room as she had hoped.

"How soon did you meet him after you fled your prison like a death row inmate who'd just been granted a stay of execution?"

Don't, Alik darling.

"H-he came to my parents' house to ask me to type a résumé for him in case he decided to work for another construction company."

"Type?"

She averted her eyes. "That's how I've been making my living. I advertised in the campus paper and the newspaper."

His mouth went taut. "How far along were you when he showed up at the door?"

I don't know, her heart moaned. "Five months."

"So you haven't spent very much time with him. He ought to be getting nervous about now." He thrust the dagger a little deeper.

Nicky's fussing prevented Blaire from having to respond. Alik was obviously torn between baiting her and taking care of his son's needs. Fortunately the baby prevailed. He wheeled around and strode through the trailer to the bedroom, taking Nicky with him.

Blaire didn't know how much longer she could live with a lie that was growing out of all proportion and would end up tearing them apart even more.

She found him on the bed holding Nicky. "Here's his bottle."

"Stay with me while I feed him. I need to talk to you."

Of necessity she stood next to the crib where she could lean against it for support. Desiring him as she did, sitting down anywhere near him was too dangerous an arena to enter.

"Look, Alik—" She spread her hands nervously. "Lane definitely overstepped his bounds but there was no harm done."

His head reared back so his eyes could gaze at her directly. "I had my chat with him. In any event you don't have to worry about him anymore because we won't be living here after this week."

The blood pounded in her ears. "What do you mean?"

"For all intents and purposes, my work in this part of the country is finished. Track can now be laid from here to Wyoming. But I have yet to study the soil in the Western half of the U.S., which means I need to relocate.

"Hannah will let us stay on her property outside Laramie for a while. She has water. We'll tow the car behind the trailer so you'll have your own transportation after we get there.

"I'd like to leave bright and early Monday morning. That gives us the weekend to houseclean this trailer of the things I don't need."

Blaire turned away from him feeling quite ill.

"I'm sorry if the idea sounds repugnant to you, but you've always known that the nature of my work keeps me on the go."

"You don't understand, Alik," she murmured. "It's one thing to carry on this charade at the site among virtual strangers, but to have to be with your best friends, to have to live in the same town with them when they must have such a horrible impression of me... I—I don't think I could handle it."

"You mean you can't last a few more weeks." His mild tone was the last straw. "No one's putting a gun to your back, Blaire. You're welcome to leave for the airport and fly home to your fiancé right now if that's what you want. Nicky and I will be happy to drive you."

She blinked back the tears so they wouldn't fall. "I could never give him up, you know that."

"Then there's no problem," he said in a satisfied voice. "I'll stay in here with Nicky and put him to bed for the night. You're welcome to use the computer to e-mail Rick. I meant to tell you that the other day."

"His modem's not working."

"That's too bad. At least you can pick up the phone if you want to hear his voice."

A change in the subject was desperately called for. "I'm going in the other room to work on Nicky's baby book." That is if the nausea passed.

"Did I tell you some of those pictures could be my mother at his age? If it weren't for the quality of the film, you wouldn't be able to tell the difference in a couple of them."

The mention of his mother made her so frightened, she knew she was going to be sick to her stomach. It was a good thing the bathroom was only a few steps away. She shut the door, then proceeded to lose her dinner.

"Blaire?" The alarm in his voice sounded genuine.

"I—I'm all right."

She rinsed her mouth, then brushed her teeth. When she emerged minutes later, he was standing next to the crib where he'd put Nicky. His features had formed a strong grimace.

"Why didn't you tell me you were sick?"

"I didn't know. It came on so fast."

"You're going to bed. I'll take care of everything. Do you need help undressing?"

Alik's anger she could stand. His tenderness was something else again.

"No, thank you. I think I'm just going to lie here for a minute until the worst of the nausea passes."

"Do you want me to take Nicky?"

"Yes, please," she whispered.

A long silence ensued. "Good night. Call out if you need anything."

I need *you*.

He picked up the baby and left the room. She noticed he left the door ajar after he turned out the light.

Weakened by the sudden sick spell, she closed her eyes for a moment, thinking she would get up in a few minutes to undress. The next thing she knew it was three in the morning. She could hear Nicky starting to fuss for his bottle. It took him a while to work up to a full-bodied cry.

Feeling much better, she slid off the bed, still dressed. Since her arrival, Alik had been up every night taking care of their son. Though he would never let on, she knew he had to be exhausted. It was her turn to give him some relief.

Deciding not to turn on any lights, she traversed her way through the dark to the playpen.

"Oh!" she cried softly when her body collided with Alik's hard-muscled physique. His arms went around her to keep them both from falling.

"What are you doing up?" His husky voice, deepened by sleep, sounded curiously intimate. He still hadn't relinquished his hold of her. When his hands roamed over her back the way they used to do, her heart hammered so hard, he couldn't help but feel its pounding against his chest.

"I—I thought it was time you had an uninterrupted night for a change."

"You're not sick anymore?" She could feel the warmth of his breath on her cheek. His mouth was dangerously close to hers. If she turned her head the slightest degree...

"No. It passed."

Knowing he probably wasn't wearing anything beneath his robe, she started to panic and pulled away from him to grab Nicky. Thank heaven she was dressed.

"As long as we're both up, I'll warm his bottle and bring it to you in your bed. How does that sound?"

No. You'd better not do that. "F-fine." She kissed Nicky's curls. "Come on, sweetheart. By the time I change you, daddy will be in."

Prophetic words. As soon as she'd settled on the bed with Nicky cradled in her arm, Alik appeared in the room. He walked over and sank down on the mattress next to her. His proximity made her breathing grow shallow.

"Here's some iced tea with lemon for you." He put the glass in her free hand.

"Thank you."

"You're welcome. And now for your midnight snack, young man."

To Blaire's shock, he held the bottle for the baby who was his noisy, hungry self.

She could sense Alik's eyes on her in the darkness. "How does that taste?"

"Divine."

"Good. Drink all of it. I don't want you to dehydrate."

Terrified to be this close to him, she swallowed the contents as fast as she could. Their hands brushed as she handed the empty glass back to him. He was supposed to stand up and go away now. But he didn't do either. Instead she felt him put the glass on the floor. He intended to stay right where he was and finish feeding Nicky!

Her heart wasn't hammering anymore. It was thudding.

"Alik—"

"Yes?"

"I—I'm feeling much better. Why don't you go back to bed. I'll put Nicky down."

"As long as I'm here, I don't mind. I think he likes having both of us this close to him in the dark. It makes him feel secure and loved."

Her cheeks were on fire. "Will you pull the bottle away now? He needs to be burped."

Whether the baby had drained all his formula or not, Blaire had to do something to break the spell Alik was weaving. She would keep Nicky against her shoulder until he fell asleep.

Still Alik remained. She felt him lift a hand to rub the back of the baby's head. "He's a miraculous creation, Blaire."

Her squeezed lungs gulped in air. "I know."

"How long were you in labor?"

"About forty-eight hours."

"That must have felt like an eternity. Did you suffer a lot of pain?"

"Not really, not after I got to the hospital and they medicated me."

"Was Rick there with you the whole time?"

Oh, no.

"No. He was working a construction job out of town."

"So who was there to help you through your ordeal?"

"My parents a-and Aunt Diana."

"If I'd had any inkling, you know I would have been there for you." His hand had drifted to her cheek. Her body ignited as she felt his thumb make ever-widening circles until it brushed the contour of her lips.

"I know," she said shakily, turning her head toward the baby's to evade his marauding fingers. But with every caress, she drowned in sensation after sensation, unable to cry out in protest. His touch had reduced her to small moans. He got up and took Nicky from her. After placing the baby gently in his cot, he returned to the bedside.

She heard him mutter something unintelligible before his mouth closed over hers, smothering those little sounds as he drove her back against the headboard.

Swamped by an ecstatic euphoria, she responded to the onslaught of his demands, helpless to do otherwise. The taste and feel of his mouth fed her desire until she was writhing in pleasure. With unmatched mastery, he sucked her into a whirlpool of longing. Deeper and deeper. She lost all cognizance of her surroundings.

Not until the baby started to fuss did she tear her lips from Alik's, horrified to discover what could have happened if she'd allowed things to continue.

Dear God. "N-Nicky needs to finish his bottle."

"I agree," he murmured. "Afterward we'll finish what we started."

"No, Alik! Whatever went on should *never* have happened! But maybe it was inevitable since we never had c-closure. Let's just consider that this was our final goodbye."

"You call that goodbye?" he mocked dryly. "I wonder how happy your fiancé would be to learn that I was the recipient of all that sexually charged energy just now."

"You're the one who kissed me." Her voice trembled.

"Why didn't you tell me to get out of the room? I was waiting."

"I didn't want to frighten Nicky."

"I don't believe you."

"You think I enjoyed that?" she cried out, hot-faced.

"I know you did," he muttered deep in his throat.

"You're wrong. I kissed you back because I felt sorry for you, for the way I ran off without facing you. Only a child acts like that. You deserved more than that from me."

"I like the way you made up for it," he whispered. "I'm looking forward to more of the same treatment once our little guy is put away for the night."

"Then you'll have to use force. I never thought you were that kind of man. But as I told you when I broke our engagement, I'm too young and inexperienced to handle a man like you."

The missile she'd fired found its target. She felt him back away from her emotionally as well as physically.

The last thing she ever wanted to do was hurt him

more. But if he touched her again, then he would know everything was a lie and his world would be forever destroyed. She would do anything to prevent that from happening.

He got up from the bed. "So you picked one you could walk all over. You're not in love with Rick!" he chided. "What's beginning to worry me is that Nicky's going to grow up realizing his mother is incapable of adult love. It's entirely possible he'll hold you accountable for that one day.

"It might be better if I retain full custody. I may be a single father, but it wasn't by choice. At least that's forgivable.

"Think about it…"

CHAPTER SIX

LAST night Alik had told her he would use Saturday as a time to sort through his paraphernalia and separate everything into piles, some to keep, others to toss. But he was so enchanted with Nicky, he stopped every so often to play with him and feed him his bottle.

As she washed the lunch dishes, Blaire cast many glances in their direction. Every time she saw Nicky respond with a smile and start wiggling excitedly, her heart melted. If anyone were to watch—who had no idea what was going on—they would assume the three of them were a blissfully happy family without a care in the world.

But the news that they were going to relocate to Laramie had kept her tossing and turning the rest of the night. Not for one minute did she believe Alik couldn't have waited until the thirty days were up before he moved them halfway across the country to Wyoming.

She feared this sudden desire to pull up stakes stemmed from a desire to humiliate her in front of his best friends. How cruel of him to put her in such a wretched position. In fact it wouldn't be that comfortable for the Giraud's, either. Close friends exchanged confidences.

Couldn't he see this action would force them to put on a good front to her face, while deep down they probably despised her for hurting Alik. In her mind the whole idea was untenable, but Alik had the upper hand. Somehow she would have to find the strength to tough it out.

It wasn't going to be easy. Other people around meant more questions. More lies to answer those questions. Once again Rick would be at the forefront of conversation.

When she'd first conceived the idea of a fiancé to throw Alik off the scent, she never dreamed it would come back to torment her like this. After Nicky was born, all she could think about was telling Alik he had a son. Little did she know he would turn this around in such a way she'd be forced to wear a straitjacket of his own special design.

While she started to make a spice cake for dinner, she noticed him put the baby back in the playpen and pick up one of the boxes he'd filled.

"I'm going to give this to Dr. Fawson," he announced without looking at her. "I'd take Nicky with me, but it's too cold and rainy out. I'll be back shortly. Lock the door behind me."

In an economy of movement, he hefted the box with apparent ease before leaving the trailer. But his sudden disappearance caused Nicky to burst into tears. It was the first time she'd seen the baby do that. Alik would be thrilled to know his son hadn't wanted him to leave.

"It's okay, sweetheart. He'll be right back." She rushed over to the playpen and picked him up.

Relieved to be alone for a little while, she walked Nicky to the door so she could turn the key in the dead bolt. Then she sat down with him on the couch and reached for the cell phone.

At this point she needed to hear a loving voice.

Being Saturday, her parents would be home. Alik's plan to leave New York wouldn't have the same impact on them as it had on her, but she wanted to keep them informed of her situation nonetheless.

After making herself comfortable, she was startled when the phone rang in her hand. The caller ID displayed the name of the long distance phone service Alik used. Thinking it must be a courtesy call of some kind, she answered it while trying to quiet her fussy baby by giving him kisses.

"Dr. Jarman's residence."

A definite silence met her ears. She could hear breathing on the other end. A strange sense of foreboding alerted Blaire's senses.

"What do you mean, Dr. Jarman's residence? Who is this?"

Alik's mother!

Blaire would recognize the peremptory tone of that brittle female voice anywhere.

Icy fingers closed around her lungs to cut off her breathing. Last night's illness was nothing compared to the way her heart thudded sickeningly in her chest.

Her first reaction was to click off, but that would send up a red flag like nothing else. The palms of her hands turned clammy while she sought inspiration.

Why didn't I just let it ring?

Nicky could always tell when she was upset. His whimpers grew louder. She rocked him back and forth, praying he would stop making noises.

"T-this is Ms. Hammond. Dr. Jarman left a few minutes ago, but he'll be right back." She tried to make her voice sound official.

"What are you doing in his trailer?"

Blaire's tension was so acute, she held the baby too tightly. He started to cry.

"I—I'm his new secretary."

After a pregnant pause she said, "He doesn't have one!"

Her hand almost crushed the phone. "I was h-hired a week ago."

"I don't believe it!" His mother was livid. "What's a baby doing there? Don't tell me he's allowing you to bring it to work with you?" she demanded, sounding furious, and worse, scandalized.

It was no use bouncing Nicky against her shoulder. Blaire couldn't get him to quiet down. He sensed something was wrong with his mommy and was reacting in the only way a baby knew how.

This conversation needed to end. "May I give Dr. Jarman a message? He'll return your call as soon as he comes back."

There was an ominous silence coming from the other end of the wire. "What did you say your name was?"

Had she recognized Blaire's voice?

Her mouth went completely dry. Though Nicky was crying at the top of his lungs, fear had immobilized her. It was in this traumatized state that Alik reappeared. One look at her frozen condition and lines darkened his striking features.

"Oh—here he is. J-just a moment."

As she started to hand him the phone, it fell from her fingers. In a deft masculine move typical of him, he picked it up before she could, his green eyes asking the question he hadn't verbalized.

"It's your mother," Blaire mouthed the words. "Please don't give me away," she beseeched him before grabbing Nicky's bottle and running to the bedroom.

Shutting the door with her backside, she paced the tiny space not taken up by the beds. After a few minutes Nicky quieted down and drank the rest of his bottle. But the whole time his gaze was focused on her face as if he didn't trust her not to get upset again.

"Oh, Nicky, Nicky," she whispered, kissing the top of his curly head. "I'm so afraid. I've got to think of a way to alter the situation before matters get any worse. Help me, sweetheart."

This was the second time within twelve hours that something to do with the mere mention of Alik's mother had made Blaire's face lose color. Not immune to her plea, he put the phone to his ear.

His black brows still furrowed in puzzlement, he said hello.

"At last, darling. It practically took an act of Congress to track you down!"

She sounded all worked up, her usual condition. *What in the hell had she said that had turned Blaire inside out?* When he'd left the trailer a little while ago, nothing that he could recall had disturbed their undeclared state of war.

Last night Blaire had looked so damn beautiful and appealing sitting there on the bed holding their son, the need to know just how great a hold Rick had on her had provoked Alik into kissing her.

He should have left it alone. Fool that he was, he knew better than to get anywhere near her. But where Blaire was concerned, he'd always been the one out of control.

Sure enough, his experiment had proved she wasn't

capable of loving any man. But once again it had backfired on him. Those smoldering embers, which had lain dormant over the last year, burst into a conflagration no amount of cold showers could extinguish.

"Mother?" he said impatiently. "How are you?"

"If you ever bothered to call, then I wouldn't have to spend half my day trying to locate you in that hovel you call *home*."

They'd been over this ground too many times in the past. "Anything else wouldn't suit my needs. Why are you calling?"

"Do I have to have a reason to talk to my favorite son?"

From childhood he'd begged her not to call him that. One day she'd slipped and said it within his older brother Reed's hearing. The fallout from that unforgivable blunder had created a whole new world of pain for everyone.

In families that weren't dysfunctional, a question like the one she'd just asked would never come up. To Alik's bitter regret, their family was anything but normal. Christine, his spoiled older sister, was a carbon copy of their mother, but with such a pretentious role model for a parent, Alik supposed it was inevitable.

He rubbed the back of his neck absently. "You always do."

She ignored his comment. "Your uncle Colin is in New York on business. He and your father are out on the golf course right now. Speaking of your father, in case you needed a reminder, it's his birthday a week from today."

"I'm aware of that," he snapped. "Is there anything else?"

"You don't have to snap my head off, Alik. Of course there's something else. I'm planning a big party for the occasion and expect you to be there."

"I'm afraid I won't be able to make it."

"You have to be here! What will everyone think?"

"I don't have to do anything, Mother. By now I thought you realized I don't respond to threats."

"Your father misses you."

"I doubt it. In any event, it's too late for that now."

"If you had any filial concern, you would stop this nonsense and come home where you belong."

His mother's manipulations couldn't touch him no matter how much she threatened or cajoled. Alik's father was the only person who had the power to rectify the situation. But at a very early age, his parent must have lost the ability to feel much of anything. Certainly he wasn't capable of giving Alik the only thing he required.

Turning on his heel, he darted a glance at the closed door of the bedroom. God willing, Alik's son would have Alik's unqualified love if nothing else!

"If that's everything, I have to go."

"No, it's not!" she cried in a strident voice. "I want to know about that woman who answered your phone."

"She's part of the staff. Why do you ask?"

"I raised you to behave more circumspectly than that, Alik. You're a single man with the Jarman name to consider. What on earth are you doing allowing that creature and her baby to work inside your trailer?

If you carry on this way, people are only going to assume the worst.''

He let out a resigned sigh. His mother would never change. ''That creature—'' he said the word with heavy sarcasm ''—is the only person who can do the job I require.''

In the motherhood department, he had to admit Blaire took top honors. For all her sins, he'd never seen a woman more in love with her baby. Considering the side of her nature that couldn't remain true to one man, her devotion to their son was nothing short of a revelation to him.

Christine ought to take lessons from Blaire. His sister couldn't have functioned without a nanny to accompany her home from the hospital with her baby. But Alik and his siblings had been raised by a string of nannies, so what could he expect?

''That's ridiculous. You've never required a secretary before. If she's so necessary, then she should be installed in another trailer separate from yours. I won't stand for it, Alik!''

''You don't have to,'' he answered in a calm voice. ''Next week I'm leaving for Laramie and won't be living here again. End of problem. Is there anything else before I hang up?''

''Are you taking that woman with you?'' She never gave up.

His jaw hardened. ''Goodbye, Mother. It's been good talking to you too.''

He clicked off the phone and headed straight for the bedroom. His unannounced entry startled Blaire who'd been walking Nicky. At the sound of the door opening, she jerked her head around.

Thankfully the baby was asleep against her shoulder. For a little while Alik would be able to talk to her without the added distraction of taking care of their son's needs.

"What did my mother say to you on the phone earlier?"

She started to back away from him. "N-nothing."

"Don't lie to me, Blaire."

"I'm not!"

Whenever she lifted that softly rounded jaw of hers in defiance, it meant she was hiding something from him.

"When you told me she was on the phone, you looked as sick as you did last night after I mentioned mother's baby pictures. I want an explanation if we have to stand here for the duration."

He watched her bite the soft underside of her lip. For one heart-stopping moment he would sell his soul for the same privilege, *if* he thought she loved him.

"A-all right," she stammered. "Your mother was a trifle cross with me because of her disappointment in not being able to talk to you right away."

"*How* cross?" he persisted.

"Alik—naturally she was surprised because you've never had a secretary before. Your mother's a very proper woman. She was probably thinking what everyone thinks who knows I'm living with you. I— I'm sure it came as a shock."

"I'm a thirty-six-year-old man who's been living on his own for years. She should have gotten over being shocked eons ago."

"Nevertheless you're not just any man." Her voice caught. She averted her eyes. "You're her baby, just like Nicky's mine. She thinks you're perfect. I also happen to know you're her favorite child."

Alik saw red.

"Did she tell you that in so many words when I flew you to New York last winter?"

He had to wait a long time. Finally Blaire gave an almost imperceptible nod of her auburn head.

"Damn her!"

Blaire's cheeks filled with hectic color. "Don't talk about your mother that way, Alik. She adores you!"

But he was beyond listening to Blaire.

"What kind of a parent tells her child a thing like that in front of her other children?"

In an instant Blaire's eyes glazed with tears. She shook her head incredulously. "Your mother did that?"

Alik struggled to contain his emotions. "Estelle Jarman has never been known for her tact. A rogue elephant has better instincts. Needless to say my brother has never been the same since."

"So *that's* why you couldn't get him to do things with us while we were there," she murmured.

Her sorrowful expression broke through his defenses. When she looked like that, he felt crucified all over again by her betrayal. It had seemed so out of character at the time, and appeared that way even more so now.

"What else did she say that put the fear in you?"

"I don't know what you mean?"

"The hell you don't!"

His angry retort caused the baby to open his eyes and look around before he moved to her other shoulder and settled back to sleep once more.

Blaire flashed Alik a look of pleading. "Can we not talk about this right now?"

"I'll drop it as soon as you answer my question,"

he muttered in a low voice of barely restrained violence.

She kept smoothing her hand against the baby's back. The gesture betrayed her nervousness, arousing his curiosity to a greater degree than ever.

"When I broke up with you, I can only imagine how she felt about me. A mother tends to champion her child, especially one who loves her son the way she loves you.

"Hearing a woman answer your phone had already given her one upset for the day. I—I don't think I could have handled her anger had she found out I was the person pretending to be Ms. Hammond. You didn't tell her, did you?"

His breath caught in his lungs. "No."

"Thank God. That would have been bad enough, but if she had realized it was our son who was crying his heart out into the receiver, then it would have given her even more reason to be hurt for you.

"Look, Alik—I realize at some point your parents are going to have to know about Nicky. But I don't think today was the right time for her to find out. You can see my reasoning about this, can't you?"

Yes. He could see.

But he saw something else in Blaire's reaction last night. It had nothing to do with today's unexpected phone call. In his gut he knew there was more to this than she was telling, but he decided to let it alone. For now.

"I have more work to do."

"So do I." She sounded infinitely relieved.

After raking a hand through his hair, he went back to the living room to finish the task he'd started.

*   *   *

When Blaire put Nicky into his crib, her body was trembling so badly, she had to hold on to the railing until strength returned to her limbs.

The experience on the phone was such a close call, she didn't think she could live through another one. Alik might consider this was the end of the trouble for now, but she had the nagging fear his mother had found the sound of Blaire's voice too familiar to let go of any suspicions in that corner. If that were the case...

She found Alik in the other room packing his journals. "Do you want some help?"

His dark head reared back. "Why?"

Nothing she said or did escaped his scrutiny. "Another pair of hands can cut the workload in half."

"And?" He fired the operative word at her.

It was frightening how easily he read her mind. "I—I thought maybe we could leave for Laramie tomorrow instead of Monday."

His lips twisted savagely. "For someone who almost went into cardiac arrest last night because I told you we would be relocating to Hannah's property, your suggestion that we get out of here as soon as possible doesn't exactly add up."

What can I say to you that won't make you think I'm running from your mother?

"Maybe it's because at home I could take long walks along the beach. The first time I tried to get a little exercise around here, it didn't work out. The drive to Laramie isn't the same thing of course, but the idea of getting out in the wide-open spaces, of seeing the countryside sounds very appealing."

"I'm afraid the truck won't be ready to go until Monday morning. However since I'm feeling rather restless myself, why don't we take the night off and drive into Warwick to see a movie tonight.''

It sounded like heaven except for one thing. ''We can't take Nicky.''

''True, but maybe I can fix that.''

She stood there in astonishment as he looked up a number in the directory, then made a phone call. In a minute he was arranging for hotel accommodations and a sitter.

After clicking off, he turned to Blaire. ''It's all set. We have a room with two queens and a crib for tonight. Mrs. Wood, the woman who tended for you before, will be happy to watch Nicky. She'll be free to come to our room by seven.''

It sounded too much like a date. She was too excited. ''I—I'd enjoy that,'' she murmured, not looking at him. ''Do you want to have dinner here before we leave?''

''No. Let's make an evening of it. Why don't you shower now, then there'll be enough hot water for me after I finish packing the rest of the boxes. Wear something dressy. I feel like French cuisine tonight.''

When Blaire had packed for the trip to Warwick, she hadn't planned on her life going in an entirely different direction after her arrival. She certainly hadn't packed the kind of attire he seemed to have in mind.

''I'm afraid all I have is the cotton sweater and skirt you saw me in that first morning.''

''That's fine. I thought we might both enjoy a change.''

No doubt he was sick of seeing her in the same two pitiful outfits she'd brought with her. Never dreaming she would be spending time with him, she'd only brought two of her most casual jeans and a couple of T-shirts.

Four hours later they put everything in the car needed for their overnight stay. After Alik had strapped Nicky in his infant seat, Blaire had trouble taking her eyes off him.

Any kind of clothes looked wonderful on Alik, but tonight he took her breath away in a tailored, olive-toned wool suit with a cream shirt and striped tie. Having come fresh from the shower, the scent of the soap she always associated with him emanated from his side of the front seat.

As they drove into Warwick, the ache she'd been living with for close to a year grew acute. When they walked through the hotel lobby to the elevator, every woman in the vicinity stared openly at Alik. But he was so busy showing off his son, he seemed oblivious to the female attention that followed him everywhere he went. Not so Blaire who felt like scratching their eyes out.

It killed her to think that once upon a time she'd worn his diamond, impatiently waiting to become his bride. But his mother had transformed that starry-eyed girl into a wraith who was forced to slither into the shadows and disappear.

All Mrs. Jarman had had to say was, "Out damn spot!"

How irate Alik's mother would be to see that the damned "spot" was back. Blaire happened to glance at Nicky just then. "Two spots," she amended inwardly.

Once in their hotel room, no one could have acted more pleased to be of use than Mrs. Wood who eyed Alik in admiration and greeted Nicky as if he was her own little grandson. Alik seemed gratified by the older woman's response. When she told them to stay out as long as they wanted, he said he planned to take her up on it.

Later, over wine and chateaubriand for two, a change from his usual preference for seafood, Blaire began to feel as if she was that besotted fiancée once more. In fact when he raised his wineglass in a toast to Nicky, she smiled into his beautiful green eyes and touched her glass to his.

"To our handsome son. May he grow up to be as remarkable as his wonderful father."

But her euphoria changed to panic when her gaze happened to catch the glint from her aunt's diamond ring, reminding her she was supposed to be engaged to someone else.

Too late she realized her mistake.

Lowering her eyes from the enigmatic gleam she could see between his dark-fringed lashes, she said, "You know? I'm feeling a little dizzy. Maybe it's because I haven't had any alcohol since before I conceived. I'm afraid it's gone to my head. It might be best if I went outside for a breath of fresh air."

She'd made up the business about the wine as an excuse to cover her unwise behavior. But when she got up from the table, she swayed in place.

In an instant Alik had grasped her upper arms to help steady her. He felt so good. More than anything in the world she wanted to burrow into his male strength and never let go. But she didn't dare.

"Easy does it."

He placed a hundred-dollar bill on the table, then escorted her from the restaurant where she could inhale gulps of air. Anything to clear her head so she wouldn't lose control like that again.

"The theater's only a block away. Let's walk."

Incapable of speech, she moved with him, trying desperately not to make contact. But occasionally her hip brushed against his, striking fire each time until she feared she might explode in flame.

The techno thriller appeared to absorb Alik. In Blaire's case, she couldn't get into it. But at least she was no longer in that bemused state of saying and doing things she would live to regret.

By the time the film was over, Blaire had regained her equilibrium and could walk back to the car without his help. For so long she'd been using Nicky as a shield against Alik's charisma, she felt at a complete loss without him.

The second they reached the hotel room, she made a beeline for her son who was sleeping soundly in the crib. She wanted to pick him up, but not while the older woman was still there.

"Thank you for watching Nicky, Mrs. Wood."

"He's a darling. I hope you'll call me again."

Blaire refrained from saying anything. What could she say? *This isn't what you think. This man is not my husband. After a few more weeks, we'll never be this close to each other again.*

"The next time we're in Warwick, you can count on it," Alik assured the retired nurse.

There won't be a next time, her heart cried.

"Blaire? I'm going to see her out to her car. I'll be right back."

One of the things she loved most about Alik was his thoughtfulness. "All right. Good night, Mrs. Wood."

"Good night."

As soon as they left the room, Blaire made certain the baby was comfy, then she flew into the bathroom to get ready for bed. Throwing her robe on over her nightgown, she climbed under the covers and reached for the cell phone lying on the nightstand. It was imperative Alik believe she'd used the time he was gone to talk to her fiancé.

When he returned a few minutes later, she was lying on her side away from the door with the phone next to her ear.

He walked over by her bed and stood there. She could feel his piercing glance. Swallowing hard, she turned in his direction to let him know she realized he'd come back in the room. His grim countenance prompted her to end her fake phone conversation in a hurry.

"I have to go now, Rick. I'll talk to you tomorrow. I love you, too."

She clicked off, then pretended to clear the log before she put his phone back on the table.

Daring to look up once more, she winced to see that his features had become an expressionless mask.

"You haven't slept in a real bed for a week, Alik. I'll get up with Nicky in the night so you can take advantage of it. Before I say good night, let me thank you for a lovely evening. It was exactly the change I needed."

"I'm glad to hear it. Since you've opted to take care of our son, then I don't suppose you'll mind if I don't come to bed for a while."

Her heart plunged to her feet to watch him disappear out the door.

Where was he going?

Prior to her arrival, he'd been living outside Warwick for several months. During that amount of time he could have met any number of willing women. He might even have been in a relationship with one of them when Blaire appeared on the scene. Maybe he still was.

When she really thought about it, he'd been more than eager to get away from the trailer for the night. Giving Blaire an evening out at a hotel with the baby was the perfect way to kill two birds with one stone.

She couldn't bear it.

CHAPTER SEVEN

ALIK ignored the come-on from the attractive blonde seated at the bar and found himself a table in the corner of the dimly lit room. Most of his adult life he'd avoided bars. He found them depressing places. To him they represented a refuge of last resort.

He hadn't come into the hotel bar to drink. When the waiter approached him, Alik asked for a ginger ale and a phone.

It was eleven-thirty Utah time. Hopefully Zane hadn't gone to sleep yet. Even if he had, Alik needed to talk. On the tenth ring his friend picked up.

"Alik! You don't usually call this late unless it's personal. What's on your mind?"

"I'm moving the trailer to Laramie next week."

"You already told me that. How's your little acorn?"

He closed his eyes. "Nicky's the only thing in this whole damn mess that makes any sense at all. I had no idea what it meant to love a child until I held him." His voice shook.

"You're a lucky guy. I'm looking forward to seeing him. As soon as you get to Wyoming, give me a ring and I'll fly out. Now let's talk about Blaire. What's going on, bud?"

"Hell, Zane. I wish I knew. Just when I think I've got her figured her out, she does something that rips my guts apart all over again."

"You know something? I'm probably the wrong

person to talk to. Both times I was engaged, I couldn't bring myself to get married and felt nothing but relief when I walked away.''

"Obviously neither woman was the right one for you. At least you had the guts to call it quits before lives were ruined. I wish I felt the way you did. I'd like to be able to tell Blaire to go to hell, then run in the other direction without wanting to look back.''

"Is she still responsive to you?''

His mind relived the experience in the trailer bedroom. "Yes.''

"And she's planning to marry this other dude next month?'' He sounded as outraged as Alik felt.

"That's the hell of it. I don't think she knows what real love is. The longer I'm with her, the more I'm becoming convinced she's too immature emotionally to commit to a permanent relationship. Of course that's what she's been telling me all along, but I haven't wanted to believe it.''

"Is she a good mother to your son?''

"She's unbelievable. That's why I don't understand this other side of her.''

"Are you sure she's getting married?''

"She's wearing his ring. I heard her on the telephone earlier. She told him she loved him.'' He thought he couldn't feel any more pain. But he'd been wrong.

"Have there been any signs of preparation? Is she making lists and doing all those thousand and one details fiancées do to get ready for the big day?''

Alik blinked. "No. At least not in my presence.''

"I think you would notice. That kind of stuff is pretty impossible to miss.''

"She has my baby. In all probability she and Rick have decided to get married without any fanfare."

"Are you going to be able to handle that?"

"I don't know. I told you about the bargain I made with her. So far she's kept her part of it to the letter. I told her that if her fiancé stepped foot inside the trailer, then our contract was null and void. He hasn't been near. Which means I'll have to honor my part.

"But if we're going to share custody, one of us will have to move in order to be with Nicky on a full-time basis."

There was a long pause. "I can't see you setting up a base in San Diego. That place holds too many memories for you."

"Tell me about it," Alik ground out. "But I doubt Blaire's fiancé is willing to make the sacrifice. So it seems that if I want to have a solid relationship with my son, I don't any choice but to live in California."

"Alik?"

He cleared his throat. "Yes?"

"Before you make any assumptions, you should ask to meet Rick."

"Why? It wouldn't do any good. The guy's going to need all the contacts he can think of to line up construction jobs. Moving to a strange place where he doesn't know a soul would be disastrous for him financially."

"Hey, bud—you misunderstood me."

Alik frowned. "What do you mean?"

"I mean, have a one-on-one with him about Nicky, and find out just how much he still wants to marry Blaire knowing you'll be in their lives all the time. If he's not mature enough to handle that, it could frighten the guy off.

"In that case, you'll be saving Blaire the grief of going through the motions of a wedding, only to have it crumble afterward. Ultimately it will be better for Nicky."

After Zane's wisdom had sunk in, Alik felt galvanized into action. He rose to his feet and put some money on the table.

"You know something, Zane? For a man who told me you're the wrong person to talk to, you've made the most sense out of this mess since I found Blaire in my trailer.

"After she and I are settled in Laramie with the baby, I'm going to take your advice and fly out to San Diego for a serious talk with her fiancé."

Zane made a gratified sound in his throat. "It certainly can't hurt anything."

"You're right about that. Thanks for answering the phone."

"Anytime, Alik. See you next week."

After the click, Alik gave a parting nod to the waiter, then left the bar for the hotel room. Since Nicky had come into his life, he made a habit of checking on him before he went to bed.

The baby was sleeping so quietly, Alik worried he was unconscious. But when he put the back of his hand near his precious face, he felt the warmth of his breath and realized his son was very much alive. How amazing that just over a week ago he hadn't known of Nicky's existence. Now this tiny scrap of humanity had a stranglehold on his heart as strong in its own way as that of Nicky's mother.

Much as Alik might like to go over and find out if Blaire was still breathing, he knew if he did, he would end up touching her. If that happened, then he would have to join her. In his gut he knew she would welcome him.

But she wasn't in love with him.

Now that they had a son, more than ever his heart rebelled against their coming together unless the oldest ritual known to man meant the same thing to her as it did to him. Since that wasn't the case, he was determined to avoid temptation altogether, otherwise he was in danger of losing his soul.

Terrified of that prospect, he prepared for bed without giving as much as a glance to the beautiful female body slumbering a few feet away. When he finally slid beneath the covers, he turned toward the wall and willed sleep to numb the ache.

On their drive back to the site Sunday morning, Alik talked to Blaire about their impending trip to Wyoming, which was coming up the following day. Since the journey would probably take three to four days, he thought it would be better if they stayed at motels, and ate at drive-in's and café's en route.

Blaire agreed with him. They would need to get out and stretch their legs every so often. At night she would be able to hold Nicky who would be relegated to his infant seat in the extended portion of the truck's cab during the daytime hours.

Upon their return to the trailer, Blaire changed Nicky's diaper, then got busy cleaning the fridge. She decided to throw everything out. When they arrived in Laramie, she would go to the grocery store and stock it again.

Alik had found a note from Dr. Fawson taped to the door requesting that they have a final meeting over lunch in his trailer. After hooking up the station wagon to the back of the trailer, Alik came in for a shower. When he was dressed in a burgandy-toned crew neck shirt and trousers, he told Blaire he was leaving and had no idea what time he would be back.

Since returning from town, the hostility coming from Alik seemed more pronounced than usual. Afraid to make things worse, she simply nodded her head, not stopping to pause in her work of washing the vegetable and fruit bins.

Because of the chilly atmosphere between them, his departure, no matter how brief, came as a relief. Always careful around the baby, this time he let the door slam shut. Fortunately Nicky was in his crib asleep and didn't hear the loud noise.

After a half hour, she decided Alik's meeting might turn out to take up a large portion of the day. In that event she would start packing one of the suitcases with Nicky's extra blankets and supplies they wouldn't need until they reached their destination.

When it was full, she carried it out to the trunk of the station wagon where she put it next to the stroller and musical swing. Once back inside the trailer, she looked around wondering what else she could pack right now. An unexpected tap on the door broke her concentration.

Since this was Alik's last day, she assumed it was one of the graduate students who'd come to say goodbye. Dispensing with her normal caution of finding out who it was first, she turned the key in the lock and opened the door.

She should have guessed it would be Sandy. But she came close to fainting when she saw the one person on the planet she'd hoped never to see again in her lifetime.

Alik's mother stood a few yards off, dressed in a stunning blue silk suit made more striking because of her height. She wore her glistening black hair with those artful traces of silver piled on her head. Her flawless makeup provided the perfect foil for her green eyes, which glittered at Blaire with what she could only describe as pure malice.

"Ms. Hammond?" Sandy said with a smile Blaire viewed as a genuine smirk of satisfaction. "Dr. Jarman's mother has been looking for him. I told her his secretary would know where he was since she took care of his son day and night. And everyone at the site knows Dr. Jarman doesn't go anywhere these days without his precious Nicky in tow."

Not until now did Blaire realize the extent of Sandy's jealousy. It must have been eating at her like a poison.

As for Alik's mother...

Blaire felt as if they were all acting in a daytime soap opera where their three characters, personifications of the good, the bad and the ugly, had finally been revealed. This was the moment the TV audience had been waiting for over the last year. Now all the lies, schemes and secrets were about to be uncovered so the truth would be exposed.

Since yesterday when his mother had phoned Alik, Blaire had felt this confrontation was inevitable. She just hadn't expected it to happen as soon as the next day.

"Thank you for your help, Sandy. Come in, Mrs. Jarman. Alik's having lunch with Dr. Fawson, but I assume he'll be back shortly."

His mother swept past Sandy without a word of thanks and entered the trailer. Ignoring Sandy's smug expression, Blaire followed Mrs. Jarman inside and shut the door behind her.

"Please. Sit down." She gestured to the couch.

His mother stood stock-still while her gaze made a thorough assessment of the interior. Her condescending attitude had never been more in evidence.

With most of Alik's things put away in boxes, all that remained out were Nicky's playpen and toys. A quilt here, a bottle there. His pacifier on the counter. The baby book on the table.

"Where is he?" she demanded.

"Do you mean Alik or Nicky?"

"Your bastard child."

Blaire had already been the recipient of his mother's verbal cruelty. This was nothing new. In fact Blaire would have been shocked if Mrs. Jarman had shown any sign that she'd softened over the intervening year.

For some reason she couldn't account for, a strange calm had washed over Blaire. Maybe it was because the last time they'd faced each other, Blaire hadn't been a mother who would enter a burning building to save her baby.

Taking a good strong breath she said, "Did you know a bastard means a child of dubious or inferior origins? Whether you like it or not, and I know you don't, he's part Jarman. He's the child of your favorite son's body.

"If Alik should hear you refer to his little boy as a bastard, I can promise you, you'll never see or hear from your son again in this lifetime, and probably not the next."

Her eyes narrowed on Blaire's face. If looks could kill...

Without warning she wheeled around and headed straight for the back of the trailer. Blaire didn't try to stop her.

Driven by the need for eyewitness proof, Alik's mother had come all the way from their palatial estate on Long Island to do a firsthand inspection of the child she'd heard crying on the phone.

It didn't take long for her to emerge from the bedroom, her walk not as steady as before, her complexion a little paler beneath her foundation and blusher.

She stared at Blaire so long, Blaire wondered if the older woman had suffered a stroke.

"I underestimated you before. How much money do you want?"

All it had taken was one look.

"For what?"

"To leave the baby here and disappear for good."

"How much did you bring with you?" Blaire asked in a level voice.

"Enough that if you're careful, you won't have to prostitute yourself again the way you did when you trapped my son in your mercenary tentacles."

Blaire folded her arms. "I may be a girl from the wrong side of the tracks, unfit to be seen in public with your son, but even someone as low-class and plebian as I, has needs your money won't cover."

"You haven't heard my price yet."

"I don't need to hear it, Mrs. Jarman. No amount of money is going to separate me from my baby."

Her attractive Grecian features hardened into an ugly grimace. "Alik had no comprehension of your type when he brought you home. You think you're so clever to present him with his son. But it doesn't matter. You're still not going to get your hands on one penny of his money, and you know why…"

Yes. Blaire knew why. It was the reason she'd broken their engagement and run away where Alik couldn't find her.

"Obviously it's impossible for you to believe, but I don't want or need his money. I'm getting married to someone else in less than two months."

Blaire extended her hand so Alik's mother could see the modest half-carat solitaire on her ring finger. Her aunt's diamond didn't compare to the two-carat princess cut Alik had given her, the one she'd left on his dresser when she'd fled from his family's estate.

"Rick Hammond, my fiancé, will be taking care of me and Nicky. We won't want for a thing. You see, I came to Warwick for one purpose only. To find out if Alik wanted to share joint custody of Nicky.

"A father and son have the right to know and love each other. If you saw them together now, you would realize that Alik adores Nicky, and Nicky worships his father."

Her dark head reared back angrily. "In your case, joint custody is simply another word for extortion."

"Maybe in your eyes," Blaire murmured. "Whatever Alik chooses to do with his son, however he wishes to spend his money on him, that will have nothing to do with me."

Blaire's avowal seemed to capture her attention.

"You would put that in writing for my attorney to witness?"

"Yes."

It was evident his mother was surprised Blaire had called her bluff.

"When?"

"Whenever you say."

She eyed Blaire speculatively. "You realize what it would mean if you were to go back on your word after signing a legal document."

"I broke off our engagement, didn't I." Blaire's voice throbbed with remembered pain.

"But you covered all your bases by returning with something my son wants," came the brittle riposte.

"You mean the flesh of his flesh?" Blaire cried. "It was the right thing to do. The *only* thing to do!"

"We'll see how sincere you are when you have to sign on the dotted line."

"I wish you had brought your attorney with you. I could put my signature to paper right now and have it over with."

Suppressing her pain and anger had caused Blaire's entire body to break out in perspiration. The Spanish Inquisitors had nothing on Alik's mother. Blaire prayed she would leave.

The older woman cocked her head. "You have depths I hadn't suspected were there."

I could return the compliment, but I wouldn't want you to think I was flattering you. How could a woman like you have mothered a son as wonderful as Alik?

As if thinking about him had conjured him up, Alik entered the trailer without warning, his gaze going directly to Blaire's. He sounded out of breath. For an infinitesimal second, she thought she saw a trace of anxiety in those troubled green depths before he darted his parent a questioning glance.

"Mother? Sandy told me you were looking for me. What are you doing here?"

She smiled at her son, eyeing him hungrily. "What

kind of a greeting is that? Blaire's going to wonder where your manners have gone.''

Blaire watched him give her a peck on the cheek before his hands went to his hips. ''When we talked yesterday, you didn't say anything about coming to Warwick.''

''You didn't say anything about having a son!'' she reprimanded him, but there was no sting.

Once again Blaire marveled over what a clever, manipulative woman she was.

''After we hung up, I remembered hearing that woman's voice before. It was Blaire's! Suddenly the reason why you were allowing a strange woman with a baby to live in your trailer made sense.

''When I realized it was my grandchild I could hear crying in the background, I decided to come and see him for myself.'' She clapped her hands together. ''He's the image of you when you were a baby, Alik! I can't wait until he wakes up so I can hold him!''

A soft look entered Alik's eyes. ''He's a miracle.'' The love in his voice moved Blaire to tears.

''Indeed he is,'' she concurred. ''Before you came in, I was telling Blaire I admire her honesty in letting you know about Nicky. Heavens, there are too many girls in this modern age who don't consider the birth father in these matters.

''Why Blaire could have married her fiancé and you would never have had the slightest idea he would be raising your son. When you walked in the trailer, she was just explaining that you two are in the process of working on a joint custody arrangement. That's the way it should be.

''I'm sorry things didn't work out between you last year. Obviously it wasn't meant to be. But it must please you, Alik, that your son is being raised by such an honorable woman as Blaire.''

Once again Alik's astonished-looking gaze searched hers, this time for verification.

Like last year, Blaire had no choice but to play along. ''I told your mother that I felt a father and his son should be together.''

Mrs. Jarman touched his arm. ''This is a momentous occasion, darling. Certainly the news about Nicky is too wonderful to be kept hidden from the family any longer!'' she declared with the right tone of excitement.

''Alik? Blaire has agreed to accompany you and the baby to the house next weekend for your father's birthday celebration. It will be a night to remember!''

Blaire averted her eyes. Not only had she caught sight of Alik's remote expression, but she was aghast to think she would have to set foot on Jarman property again in order to sign that document. But she'd made a promise to her. Now she had to conform to the conditions.

''I'm afraid that won't be possible, Mother. We're going to be in Laramie.''

''You can fly to New York on Saturday for the party, and return to Wyoming the next day.''

''Please, Alik,'' Blaire urged. *Please.* ''Since the day he was born, my family has had an opportunity to be around Nicky. Think how much joy it will bring your family to see him before he gets beyond the newborn stage.

''After I leave Laramie, I'll be getting ready for my wedding and won't have time for anything else. As long as I'm still helping you with Nicky, next weekend would be the perfect time to go.''

Something profound was going on inside Alik. She saw his chest heave.

"We'll see" was all he would agree to.

His mother smiled. "I know you'll be there. But I'm not going to say a word to the family. When you arrive with our grandson, it will be the best surprise birthday present your father has ever received.

"Now I'd better go. Alik, darling? Will you walk me out to the limousine? The driver's waiting to take me back to the airport."

He nodded without saying anything.

"Blaire?" his mother addressed her. "Though I never expected to see you again, I have to tell you it has been good talking to you. Motherhood obviously agrees with you."

Dumbfounded by her performance, Blaire had to finish out the scene with the same sangfroid. "Thank you. Are you sure you don't want me to wake Nicky so you can hold him?"

"Oh, no, my dear. I've had three children. When you have to get up in the night with them, it's pure heaven if they stay asleep long enough for you to accomplish something. There'll be plenty of time to get acquainted with him when you come next weekend."

She stepped forward to kiss Blaire on the cheek before exiting the trailer. Alik followed her out the door, but not before he sent Blaire an oblique look she couldn't decipher.

Now that Alik's mother had gone, Blaire felt exquisite relief. She'd faced her worst nightmare and was still alive to tell about it.

Never in her wildest dreams would she have imagined that she'd be the one begging Alik to attend a party at his parents' estate when she knew it would take an emotional toll on him. But it had to be this way in order for her secret to remain safely hidden.

At least when they flew there next weekend, he'd be taking his son with him. The immeasurable comfort he would derive from having his little boy to hold and love would more than sustain him.

Before Nicky woke up and Alik returned, Blaire gathered a clean change of clothes and hurried into the shower. She needed one badly to wash off the film of perspiration that had enveloped her the moment she'd seen Mrs. Jarman standing near Sandy, ready to do battle.

"How long was my mother here before I came in?" Alik demanded to know minutes later when Blaire emerged from the bathroom with a towel around her wet hair.

He had been standing outside the door feeding Nicky who must have heard the water running and had started to cry for a bottle. She brushed past him to walk in the kitchen with her blow-dryer.

Like a hunter, Alik's instincts were on full alert. He would be relentless until he got the answers he was searching for.

"Maybe ten minutes." Blaire's back was to him as she put the plug into the wall socket with a trembling hand.

"After the phone call from hell, I rushed back to New York to find out what had made you break our engagement and take off for who knew where. Mother always maintained no one knew you'd gone until the next afternoon. To this day she claims total innocence in the affair. Never once in the last year has she said a bad word about you."

He drew in a breath that sounded like ripping silk. "I know my mother, Blaire," his voice rasped. "This behavior was totally out of character for her then, and it's even more so now. What really went on between you two that night?"

Slowly Blaire turned around, the blow-dryer in hand. "Absolutely nothing."

He stared into her eyes, seeking to find her weakness. It took superhuman effort, but she met the intensity of his penetration head-on.

"I patently don't believe you."

Her heart pounded out of rhythm. *This is it, Blaire. If you say the wrong thing now, you'll end up destroying Alik as surely as if you were to throw a grenade in his face.*

She removed the towel. Her damp hair fell around her shoulders. "That's because you have no comprehension of how much she loves you. Now that I've given birth to Nicky, I understand that kind of love. I would do *anything* to make sure my son loves me to the grave and beyond.

"Your mother knew how deeply you were in love with me. Do you honestly believe she was going to say or do something to make you turn on her when she knew you were in your worst pain?

"Finding out we had a baby together, can you picture her maligning the mother of her grandson?" Blaire demanded tremulously.

"She wouldn't do it, Alik! Not in a million years. You're her favorite child. She wouldn't dare do anything to ruin her relationship with you."

He didn't move. He didn't even blink. "If that's true, then why do you get that terrified look in your eyes whenever her name comes up in the conversation?''

"If I've looked terrified, it's because her name reminds me of the awful thing I did to you when I broke our engagement and disappeared so you couldn't find me.''

"Where did you go?"

"To a ranch in Arizona owned by a close friend of my father's.''

At that news, a bleak look entered Alik's eyes, piercing her heart all over again.

Blaire fought the tears, but they insisted on spilling over her lashes anyway. "I—I can't believe I treated you in such a hurtful way when you had never been anything but wonderful to me. It took the experience of childbirth to make me realize how inhumane I had been to you.

"Whether you believe me or not, I cried a lot after I brought Nicky home from the hospital. I tried not to do it around him. As soon as I had made up my mind to find you and let you know you had a son, the tears didn't fall nearly as often.

"When I see you standing there holding Nicky, then I know I've done the right thing. It can't make up for the pain of the past, but I hope one day you'll be able to find it in your heart to forgive me.

"Obviously your mother has. At least enough to make me feel welcome at your parents' home for that party. When you think about it, isn't it going to be better for Nicky if he grows up without having to deal with any animosity between your family, and mine, a-and Rick's of course.

"Nicky deserves to feel comfortable with all his

relations. If everyone starts out on the right foot now, it will set a good precedent for the future.

"You know, Alik, you never did confide in me about certain problems you've had with your parents in the past. I accepted that. But whatever they were—are—it seems to me that Nicky's advent into the world ought to go a long way toward healing some of those old wounds. He's so adorable."

A brooding silence permeated the room.

If he didn't believe everything she said, he didn't seem inclined to pursue it further. Not now anyway.

Too emotionally drained to go on like this, she pressed the button and started drying her hair.

Alik gave her one last opaque glance before carrying Nicky into the living room.

CHAPTER EIGHT

HANNAH GIRAUD insisted on taking Blaire to the supermarket in Laramie to stock their trailer.

Alik watched her retreating figure with a sense of loss that told him he was in deep, deep trouble. By tacit agreement during their trip across the country, they'd stayed away from subjects that could cause pain.

Blaire had shown a genuine interest in the bullet train project, and had plied him with detailed questions he'd found himself eager to answer. One subject had led to another as they talked about the transcontinental railway and its importance in opening up the West.

They got into a conversation about the Pony Express. Eventually Alik told her how Dominic and Hannah met and their subsequent love story.

As a result, they'd spent three glorious days of driving together, enjoying the fall weather at its most moderate. With their son fastened snugly in his infant seat right behind them, Alik had experienced such a powerful sense of family, of rightness, it didn't seem possible that Blaire would only be with him just over two more weeks before she took Nicky back to San Diego to plan her marriage to Rick Hammond.

When he thought about that now, a blackness descended over him until he felt blind with pain. More than ever Zane's advice made sense. The sooner Alik had a talk with Blaire's intended and let him know exactly how involved Alik intended to be in Nicky's life, the sooner he would find out what her fiancé was really made of.

As Zane had said, some men wouldn't be able to handle the dynamics of a situation like that over an entire lifetime. As soon as he and Blaire returned from New York, Alik was determined to discover just how much Rick Hammond truly loved Blaire.

Nicky was the only reason Alik had considered attending his family's party. It certainly wasn't to honor Alik's father. But Blaire had made a lot of sense when she'd talked about putting all animosity aside for the sake of their son who would grow up with several sets of grandparents and extended family in his life.

If relationships stayed too strained, when Nicky got older he would be curious about them and ask questions. He could get caught in the middle of something ugly and end up in the same kind of agony as Alik. If history repeated itself, then Alik had learned nothing from his experience on this earth.

For the sake of his son, he had to make an attempt at behaving in a civilized manner toward his own flesh and blood.

Blaire had done a much better job in that department, but she hadn't fooled him for a second. He knew how cruel his mother could be on occasion. The pain she'd caused Reed still tormented Alik.

Since his teens Alik had realized that no woman he married would ever be good enough for Estelle Jarman. He'd explained this to Blaire before he'd flown her to New York with him to meet his family. He'd made certain she understood that his mother had a mean-spirited nature. Blaire shouldn't be surprised if his mother refused to accept her as a daughter-in-law.

Blaire's assurance that nothing his parents might say or do could affect their love, plus his parents' surprising cordiality to Blaire upon meeting her had made him feel so secure, he'd even been able to leave her with his family for a few days while he stepped into an emergency situation to cover a seminar for a friend.

If Alik's family had been in any way responsible for their broken engagement, Blaire had never intimated as much. Otherwise on Sunday why would she have urged Alik to go to New York for his father's birthday?

It was all because of Nicky.

A child had forced Blaire to grow up in ways Alik could only admire.

As he watched Dominic lovingly eyeing his ten-month-old daughter in her swing, Alik realized what a great transformation had come over his friend.

Not that Dom wasn't already one of the best men Alik had ever met when they'd joined forces with Zane in London. But little Elizabeth had turned a somewhat world-weary, cynical bachelor into a loving husband and father, adding new dimensions to Dom's sterling character.

Alik wanted to be like that. A man Nicky would always love and respect.

If Nicky grew up wanting to be something different, do something different than Alik had in mind for him, then that was the time to show his son an even greater outpouring of love and understanding.

Nicky was all Alik would have from his own body in this world. As he looked down at his son lying in the playpen staring at Elizabeth, Alik vowed he would do everything in his power to safeguard that love.

"A *franc* for your thoughts, *mon ami.*"

Alik smiled at his perceptive friend. "I was just thinking what a great father you've turned out to be."

He gave Alik a shrug reminiscent of his Gallic ancestry. "Let us hope. Two nights ago Hannah informed me we're going to have a baby. Frankly, I'm terrified!"

That was the last admission Alik ever expected to hear come out of Dom. He clapped his friend on the shoulder.

"You're a very lucky man, you know that? You've got a beautiful wife who loves you, a little daughter who adores you. And now you're both going to have a child you made together.

"Let me tell you something, Dom. Making love to Blaire, fathering Nicky, has been the most incredible experience of my life so far. But you'll never know the terror I'm feeling right now because the woman I love is planning on marrying someone else next month," he said in a ragged voice.

Beneath furrowed black brows, Dominic's intelligent eyes searched his for a long moment. "You mean you've learned nothing new while she's been living with you? Nothing to shed light on why she really ran away?"

He shook his head. "I thought my father might be at the bottom of it. But mother found out Blaire was with me and came to the trailer last Sunday to see Nicky. She even talked Blaire into bringing the baby and flying out to New York with me for my father's birthday this coming Saturday. If Blaire's willing to face my father, then it knocks my theory all to hell."

He could hear Dominic's brilliant mind going over what he'd just told him.

"Alik—have you asked yourself why a woman who couldn't get away from you fast enough last year, would go so far as to put herself in the same position again this year when she's still not married to her fiancé?"

He closed his eyes tightly. "I've done so much asking, it has become a mantra in my brain." He bit out the words. "But I still can't come up with an explanation that makes sense. Maybe she's so afraid I'll renege on our bargain, she's willing to do anything to please me."

"Not to that degree! That's exactly why none of this adds up. You and I have shared similar family problems in our backgrounds. It was a sad day when we both had to admit we wouldn't put anything past our fathers. Perhaps it's time you considered your mother in the same light?"

Dominic's last question hung in the air like a live wire. "I have. Believe me. But Blaire hasn't given me one damn clue I can run with."

"Except for the fact that she's willing to return to the scene of the crime," Dom persisted.

"It's more than that, Dom. She pleaded with me to go. Her excuse is that we should do all we can to smooth the path for Nicky's future. If my mother is holding something over Blaire, I can't imagine what it would be."

"Neither can I. When you fly to New York, you will keep your eyes and ears open, *n'est-ce pas*? As you say in English, I smell a rat. So does Zane."

"I know. We talked the other day."

"He'll be here tomorrow. Perhaps putting three

heads together like we always do to solve problems, we might receive a little inspiration for yours.''

He raked a hand through his hair. ''Sounds good to me. I could use some divine intervention about now, otherwise I don't know if I'm going to make it, Dom.''

''Unfortunately I've been where you've been and know exactly what you mean. Come on. Let's take our children for a walk around the property.''

Between the barn and the log cabin museum, Blaire could see two tall, masculine figures strolling through the sagebrush in the far distance. The starkness of the isolated Western landscape after the heavy vegetation at the site presented an amazing contrast in topography.

Here the cool air was dry and much thinner. Having lived her life at sea level, Blaire's lungs were still adjusting to the seven-thousand-foot altitude.

Dominic's blond wife, Hannah, was a beautiful, delightful, charming person who radiated happiness and boundless energy. Blaire could well understand Alik's fondness for her and her incredibly handsome, French-born husband.

Since their arrival at noon, the Girauds had been right on the spot to help. Moreover, they'd treated Blaire with nothing but the greatest kindness and respect.

Whatever their private feelings about Blaire, she and Nicky had received the same preferential treatment shown Alik. Such generosity increased Blaire's pain because she realized what she would be missing out on when she left to go back to San Diego.

''It looks like they took our babies with them,''

Hannah exclaimed as they entered the trailer with their arms full of groceries. "Quick while they're gone! Let me help you bring in the rest of the things from the car. We'll get it all put away before little mouths need to be fed. Again."

They both laughed.

Blaire liked Hannah so much already. "If you're determined about that, then I'll have to insist you and Dominic stay for dinner. Alik loves my shrimp tacos. How does that sound to you?"

"Normally I would say divine."

"Oh—then I'd be happy to make anything else you'd like."

Hannah's green eyes danced. "No—the guys love seafood. I'm the one with the problem. I just found out the other day that I'm expecting a baby."

A sound of delight came out of Blaire. "I don't think Alik knows or he would have told me."

"I would imagine Dominic has imparted the news by now," she quipped. "Anyway, I've been a little nauseous. It comes on in the afternoon and goes away around nine."

"I can relate, Hannah. Cola was my lifesaver for the first three months. Then the morning sickness passed. It's a good thing we bought a couple of six-packs this afternoon."

Hannah nodded. "My OB has given me some medicine. He said I should be feeling much better in another couple of days."

"I surely hope so."

"You don't know how glad I am you're here. This will be my first pregnancy. Since you've just been through the experience, I have about a hundred questions I want to ask."

"But I thought Elizabeth—"

"Alik didn't tell you?"

She averted her eyes. "He told me Dominic adopted Elizabeth, but I assumed she was your baby."

After a brief silence she said, "I see. Well, my sister was an unmarried teen when she conceived Elizabeth. The father ran off. To make a long story short, with my sister's blessing, Dominic and I adopted her for our own. Now my sister's happily married. One day when they're older and ready for responsibility, they hope to start a family."

Tears glazed Blaire's eyes. "How wonderful for Elizabeth. For all of you. What a lucky little girl. But the two of you must be so excited to be having a child of your own."

"We are." Hannah's voice throbbed. "I hope it's a boy. Dominic is so envious of Alik. Your little Nicky is so sweet, and every bit as gorgeous as Alik. I've caught my husband's eyes on your baby more than once. He looks at him with such longing."

"When I presented Alik with his very own baby, it was the most amazing sight I'd ever seen. Whether you have a boy or a girl, be assured Dominic will fall in love with it."

Hannah eyed her thoughtfully. "I can see a big change in Alik from the last time he was here. Being a father obviously agrees with him.

"Look, Blaire, I don't begin to know what went on between you and Alik. Certainly it's none of my business. Please forgive me if I'm getting too personal. But I have to tell you that I love Alik, and I love you for letting him know you two had a child together."

Her words found their way to Blaire's heart. She lowered her head.

"Even though Alik was hurting over your broken engagement, he has always been there for me and Dominic, even when things were so bad between us I never dreamed we would stay married.

"For you to bring Alik his son and help him to adjust to being a new father...well, it has given him a new lease on life. I realize it must be very hard to live with him right now when you're planning to be married next month. All I can say is, I admire you for dealing with a situation most women wouldn't have the courage to handle."

"Thank you," Blaire whispered. "But you're the one who deserves praise. I admire you for taking care of Elizabeth, for loving her when your sister couldn't." She had to clear her throat before she could go on. "That's such a sweet story."

"Babies are irresistible, aren't they?" Hannah sounded as emotional as Blaire.

"Yes."

"I think Dominic was putty in Elizabeth's hands the first time he held her. I swear he fell in love with her before he did me!"

"You've got a great husband."

"I know." She sniffed. "What's your fiancé like? Do you have a picture of him?"

The question brought scalding pain.

"No. I l-left my packet of photos behind. When I left for New York, I had only planned to be gone three days. R-Rick's entirely different from Alik. Listen—why don't I get you a cola and you can lie down while I start dinner."

"Let me help."

"No. Please. I want this to be my treat. Being pregnant while you're taking care of a ten month old couldn't possibly be easy. If you stay out of the kitchen, maybe the smell from the shrimps won't bother you quite as much in the living area."

So saying, Blaire handed her a cold can of cola and suggested she stretch out on the couch. "Would you like to see Nicky's baby book?"

Hannah's eyes lit up. "I'd love it!"

"It's in the bedroom. I'll get it."

When she returned with the album, Hannah said, "Dominic and I were so thrilled to see that picture of Nicky and Alik on the e-mail, we stuck it on the fridge of our apartment."

"Does your place have room for the new baby you're expecting?"

"No!" Hannah chuckled. "It's almost as small as this trailer. Hopefully our house will be built by the time the baby gets here next May."

"How exciting!" Blaire called from the kitchen as she started browning onions and green peppers in the skillet. "Where are you going to build it?"

"Right here on the property with the horses. Alik and Zane are such nomads we've asked them to build their houses on it, too. When they're ready of course. There's plenty of acreage for all of us to have our privacy."

"D-did Alik say yes?" she had to ask.

"He's thinking about it."

Blaire clutched the counter.

Don't tell me any more, Hannah. It's killing me to hear this because I'm not going to be a part of any of it.

"Did Alik tell you the bullet train will run across my property?"

"No. I had no idea."

"It's exciting to think this land was once part of the Pony Express route, and now it will be used for a revolutionary train."

"Isn't it going to require billions of dollars?"

"Oh, yes. The men have risked every penny for this project. Their entire futures are dependent upon its success. For the last month I've been traveling with Dominic trying to do my part to help, which isn't much."

Driving across the country with Alik had given Blaire a tiny taste of what it would be like to work alongside him, to join with him in this dream these remarkable men were determined to make a reality.

Hearing about the expense involved let her know more than ever that she'd done the right thing by breaking her engagement to Alik. But she'd never envied anyone in her life the way she did Hannah Giraud.

"If you'll excuse me for a minute, I'll be right back."

Blaire made it to the bathroom just in time to break down sobbing into a towel, praying it would muffle the sound.

Dominic helped clear the dinner dishes off the table. "Blaire? You're going to have to give my wife the recipe. Those are the best tacos I've ever eaten in my life!"

"Thank you," she murmured as she loaded the dishwasher. By the time everything was cleaned up, Dominic had seated himself on the couch to play with

Nicky, while Alik helped Hannah feed golden-haired Elizabeth her rice cereal and plums.

When Blaire walked in the living room, Dominic looked up. "Before it gets too dark, why don't you and Alik take a ride? He can show you where the track is going to be forged."

No. I don't dare.

"Maybe I'd better not. I—I've only been riding a couple of times in my life. I think Alik's probably too tired after the long drive tod—"

"Actually I've never felt more wide-awake," he gainsayed her, getting to his feet. "There's nothing to it, Blaire. You'll enjoy it."

"Don't worry about Nicky," Dominic added. "Hannah and I will hold down the fort. I want some time to get acquainted with this little guy. He's going to help me practice for the big event."

Blaire saw the private look he and Hannah exchanged. The love between them was tangible.

"If it feels too chilly, use my jacket, Blaire. It's hanging inside the barn."

"Thank you, Hannah."

After bending to give Nicky a kiss, she filed out the trailer door behind Alik on rubbery legs. The barn stood a short distance off. It was cold out, but the colors of the setting sun were beautiful.

Alik opened the door and went inside. When she caught up to him, he held Hannah's sheepskin jacket. Avoiding his eyes, she slipped into it. His hands on her upper arms seemed reluctant to let her go.

With pounding heart she eased away from him, and walked toward the stable out of breath.

"There's only one horse!" she cried in alarm.

"That's right," he replied in a bland tone.

"Dominic told me his stallion is at the vet. This is Hannah's mare, Cinnamon."

He reached for the bridle hanging on the wall and put the bit between the horse's teeth.

"Come stand next to me and I'll help you up. Put your left foot in my hands."

This would force the kind of closeness she'd been able to avoid up to now.

"W-why don't you ride and I'll watch."

"Don't be frightened. Cinnamon's used to me riding her. Up you go."

Before she could stop him, his hands bit into her waist and he lifted her onto the horse. Like lightning he jumped on behind her and grasped the reins.

"How did you learn to do that?" she blurted, marveling at his expertise despite her fear of his proximity.

"Hannah used to ride in the rodeo. She's a great teacher. Just lean back against me and you won't fall off. Let's go, shall we?"

He made a clicking noise. Cinnamon started walking out of the barn. When they had cleared the paddock, she broke into a gallop. With nothing to hold on to, Blaire had no choice but to let Alik support her.

They flew over the ground faster and faster. Blaire experienced a sudden rush of exhilaration she'd never known before. Alik didn't pull back on the reins until they came to the top of the ridge overlooking the river.

While Cinnamon pranced in place, Blaire felt Alik's fingers move her hair away from her shoulder. "Now that this silk is no longer hindering my vision," he whispered against her neck, "I can show you the route the track will take."

His touch reduced her limbs to water.

Perhaps it was an unconscious gesture on his part, but his left hand slid around her hip to the middle of her stomach, while his right arm brushed against her cheek as he pointed to an imaginary line running alongside the water.

It was impossible to concentrate when she could feel the wild pounding of his heart against her back. His breathing had grown as shallow as hers. His hand started to mold to her stomach, pressing her closer against him.

"*Dear God*, Blaire." His voice sounded raw with emotion. "You smell heavenly." His mouth made small forays against her neck, kissing and caressing her hot skin, driving her mad with desire.

"No—we musn't!" She gasped the words frantically as she felt him cup her chin and urge her back against his arm. "This isn't fair to Rick."

"Nicky's existence proves I once had a prior claim. I know you still want me. Let's at least be honest about that," he muttered savagely before lowering his mouth to hers.

For a few minutes her senses swam as he proceeded to kiss the breath from her body. She forgot she was on the top of a horse out in the middle of nowhere. All that was real was this man she loved with every fiber of her being.

But when she heard herself moaning in ecstasy, it brought her back to an awareness of what she was doing. Using all her strength, she pulled herself upright, breaking their kiss and the spell he'd cast over her.

She couldn't tell who was trembling the most.

"As I recall, this wasn't part of our bargain," she said disdainfully. "Now that you've gotten that out of your system, I'd like to get back to the trailer."

"By all means." There was a satisfied note in his deep, husky voice. "When you talk to Rick later tonight, send him my regards."

On their gallop to the barn, it was lucky Blaire could blame her tears on the cold breeze, which had sprung up seemingly out of nowhere. This time she was ready for Alik.

When they reached the stable and he slid off Cinnamon's back, she lowered herself from the horse's right side and ran out of the barn. Not until she'd entered the trailer, and then had to wait for the stitch in her side to go away, did she realize she was still wearing Hannah's jacket.

Both of them looked up at her from the couch at the same time, their startled gazes questioning. Dominic spoke first.

"Are you all right?"

"Y-yes. Of course."

"How was your ride?" Hannah wanted to know.

"I-it was fine. What about Nicky? Did he fuss?"

"Not at all. He's in bed sound asleep."

Her cheeks felt hot. They probably looked hot, too. Feeling like a fool, she took off the jacket and placed it on the arm of the couch. "Thank you for letting me borrow it, Hannah."

"You're welcome. Darling—" She turned to her husband. "I think it's time we left and got our little sleepyhead to bed. If you'll carry her out to the car, I'll gather everything and put it into her baby bag."

By the time Blaire had thanked them profusely for

everything, and had said good-night at the door of the trailer, Alik had locked the barn and was walking toward them. Unable to face him after what had transpired by the river, she dashed into the bedroom and got ready for bed.

With Nicky asleep, Alik had no reason to check up on him. Thankful the Girauds were keeping him entertained outside, she shut the door, turned out the light and dived under the covers.

Her heart seemed to resound in the room. She feared Alik would be able to hear it and come to investigate.

After twenty minutes, the pounding started to die down. She was just beginning to feel a measure of calm when the door opened. Alik's masculine frame was a tall silhouette against the light from the other room.

"You forgot *this*." He tossed his cell phone on her bed. "Never let it be said that I stood in the way of true love."

Zane alighted from the two-engine plane carrying an overnight bag. He strode with purpose toward Alik and Dominic who were waiting for him at the small airport.

After tossing his suitcase in the rear of the station wagon, he climbed in the back and shook both their hands, but Alik noticed their blond friend's usual smile was missing. Dom had picked up on it as well.

"What's wrong, *mon ami*?"

"I have some news," he said, gazing directly at Alik. "This has to do with Blaire. Why don't we get out of here, and then I'll tell you about it."

Alik swallowed hard, then turned on the engine and

drove them away from the tarmac to an isolated access road. After coming to a dead stop, he turned around.

"Go ahead. Tell me what this is all about."

"Yesterday I had to fly to San Diego to confer with the engineers working on those special materials they were going to ship to me, and then didn't. While I was there, I took the time to phone Blaire's parents and ask for a Rick Hammond, pretending to be a friend of his."

"What did they say?" Alik's body had gone rigid.

"They'd never heard of him. Didn't have a clue."

A groan escaped Alik's throat.

"I remembered you telling me he went to a junior college, so I phoned every college and university in the area. No Rick Hammond was ever registered at any of them."

Adrenaline spilled into Alik's bloodstream, firing his system.

"At that point I went to the motor vehicle's division and persuaded a young lady to look up his name on her computer. Alik—if Blaire's fiancé is named Rick Hammond or any close facsimile thereof, he doesn't live in San Diego or its outskirts."

Dominic's eyes narrowed. "Which means he either lives elsewhere—"

"Or he doesn't exist."

The three of them stared at one another while Alik's mind reeled at the implications.

"Lord. If she's been lying to me..."

"Then it could mean any number of things," Zane reasoned.

Alik nodded. "You're right. Zane? How do I thank you?"

"Why don't you wait to do that until you know the truth."

"I think Zane's on to something."

"So do I, Dom. If it's all right with you, I'll take you to your apartment, then I'm going back to the trailer to have it out with Blaire. The three of us can meet up later in the day. I'll phone you."

"It sounds like a plan."

A half hour later Alik drove up next to the trailer ready to do battle. Blaire looked surprised when he unlocked the door and walked in on her holding Nicky against her shoulder.

"I didn't expect you back so soon. Where's your friend Zane? Didn't he come?"

Alik was too energized to sit. He stood in the middle of the room fighting the urge to take her by the arms and shake the truth out of her.

"Yes. He came."

He noticed she hugged the baby a little tighter. "What's the matter, Alik? Why are you staring at me like that?"

"Yesterday Zane was in San Diego on business."

When the words registered, her face lost color, the first sign of a crack in the veneer.

"Do you want to tell me whose ring you're wearing? Because it sure as hell isn't Rick Hammond's. There is no Rick Hammond."

If she'd been telling him the truth, she would have immediately refuted his claim. The fact that he was met with stone-cold silence told its own tale.

"Why the fiction, Blaire?"

It seemed like an eternity before she said, "Because I didn't want you to think I'd come to New

York with the hope that you would take me back and be financially responsible for me."

Alik had wanted the truth.

She'd just given it to him.

"But you still desire me."

Blaire faced him at last. "I've never denied my attraction for you, but I have no intention of doing anything about it. When I told you I'd changed my mind about marrying you and took off your ring, I meant it.

"Since your mother is under the impression that I'm engaged to someone else, don't you think that when we attend the family party tomorrow night, it would be better if we let her go on believing it?"

When you fly to New York, you will keep your eyes and ears open, n'est-ce pas? As you say in English, I smell a rat. So does Zane.

CHAPTER NINE

ALIK grabbed a clean change of clothes and announced he was taking a shower. When he'd shut the bathroom door and turned on the water, he phoned the apartment where Hannah had been living when she'd met Dominic.

Both men got on an extension. Neither was surprised to learn there was no fiancé.

He sucked in his breath. "I'm indebted to you, Zane."

"All I did was a little sleuthing."

"A little sleuthing has taken the haze away. I'm seeing more clearly now, just as Dom said I would."

"That's very good, *mon ami.*"

"Blaire doesn't know it yet, but I'm going to drive us to Denver in a few minutes to do some shopping before our trip. We'll stay overnight at an airport hotel so we can board the early-morning flight tomorrow in good time.

"Plan to make yourself at home in the trailer, Zane. I'll leave the key to the truck and the trailer on the lintel above the barn door. The girls just stocked this place with food. Everything's at your disposal."

"I'll take you up on that."

"It's the very least I can do after everything you've done for me."

"When you get to New York, don't trust anyone," Dominic reminded him once more.

"I'm way ahead of you."

"God bless," Zane murmured.

"Amen," Dom echoed. "Just a minute, *mon vieux*—my wife wants to get in a last word."

Alik gripped his cell phone tighter.

"Alik?"

"Yes, Hannah?"

"Blaire and I had quite a little heart-to-heart yesterday. She didn't say anything revealing. It was what she wouldn't say that gave her away. At one point she ran into the bathroom and sobbed her heart out. Only a woman in love does that."

In the deepest crevices of his soul Alik wanted to believe her. But if there was no mystery to uncover with his family, and Blaire still insisted on going back to San Diego...

"Thank you for telling me that, Hannah. You're a sweetheart."

"I really like Blaire." Her voice trembled. "You know?"

Yes. I know.

Memories of the erotic kiss they'd shared last night on Cinnamon had started a forest fire.

"Talk to all of you soon. Take care, Hannah."

He clicked off the phone and started removing his clothes. Ten minutes later he emerged from the bathroom dressed and ready to set his plans into motion.

Blaire was in the bedroom changing Nicky's diaper.

"As long as you have to get him dressed again, be sure to put his blue coverall suit on, too."

She darted him a questioning glance. "Why?"

"Because we're going to spend the night in Denver. I want to get there before the shops close. I've given a lot of thought to what you said about letting go of the past for Nicky's sake. Mother's gone to the trouble to plan a big celebration for my father.

"There'll be a myriad of distinguished guests from the bank, a senator or two, heads of several foundations, relatives from England and Greece. Immediate family. Champagne. An orchestra. Dancing.

"I think if we're going to attend the party, we should do it in grand style. She'll have a photographer there. One day when Nicky sees those pictures, we'll want him to be proud of his parents.

"It will be a very dressy occasion. Mother doesn't know how to do things any other way. So we'll shop until we find something long and gorgeous for you, and the latest style of tux for me. I understand they have tuxes for babies. We'll see what we can come up with for Nicky.

"This is going to be a short trip. I have to be back by Sunday night to discuss important business with Dominic and Zane. That's why he's here.

"Therefore we won't have much to pack, except Nicky's paraphernalia of course. I'd like to be ready to drive out of here within twenty minutes."

Leaving her standing there with a stunned expression on her face, he took the keys off his ring and went outside to put them above the barn door for Zane.

For the first time in almost a year, Alik felt in control of his life again. It was an exhilarating sensation.

If Blaire could fabricate a fiancé, she was capable of fabricating other lies as well. At this precarious stage, he refused to allow doubts to cripple him. Eleven months had been long enough to wallow in grief that had left him unable to function or think.

No more!

After throwing his things together, he went back in the bedroom. "What can I do to help?"

He could tell his plans had thrown her. She wouldn't face him. In fact he hadn't seen her act this flustered and nervous since her arrival in Warwick.

"I-if you'll get Nicky settled in the car, I'll finish packing our things."

With the greatest of pleasure Alik reached for his son. "Come on, little guy. Let's give your mother some breathing room. Under certain circumstances like now, the men aren't wanted, so we'll go do our own thing. See you at the car, mommy.

"Take a look at the world around you, Nicholas Regan Jarman. See that blue sky? Breathe the fresh air? This is open country where a man and his horse have room to think. With the right kind of friends, it's the place to get your priorities in order."

He kissed Nicky's black curls. "You're going to live here with me, son. I can tell you right now, life doesn't get better than this," he muttered as his gaze narrowed on the breathtaking woman who emerged from the trailer a few minutes later struggling with two suitcases and a diaper bag.

He settled Nicky in the back of the station wagon, then relieved Blaire of her burden. Once everyone was strapped in, they were off.

Without a lot of tourists on vacation, the freeway from Cheyenne to Denver wasn't nearly as crowded. They got to their destination with time to spare.

When they'd parked next to the mall, Alik pulled the stroller out of the back and made Nicky comfortable. "I think we'll get your mommy's shopping done first. Women have a lot more decisions to make than men."

Blaire remained suspiciously quiet as he headed for a particular dress shop he'd passed on other visits. It sold evening wear of a renowned Italian designer he'd love to see on the reluctant woman keeping her distance at his side.

Ignoring her reticence, he entered the exclusive shop and asked the clerk if she had something to match Blaire's eyes. The older woman surveyed Blaire with a critical gaze, then said she would return.

When she came back a few minutes later, she was carrying a dress that stopped him in his tracks.

It was an original two-piece, full-length evening gown of shimmering pearl-gray velvet with three-quarter sleeves and a draped neckline. Like Blaire's eyes, the lightweight fabric had a crystalline quality.

The line would be sensational on her body, especially the way the hem of the top would drape around her hips. With her auburn hair left long and flowing, she would captivate every eye and be in exquisite taste.

He knew the kind of crowd his mother would assemble. The women would all be in designer clothes. Alik couldn't care less if Blaire showed up in a sack, but for her sake he wanted Blaire to know she was the best dressed woman there to boost her confidence.

"I'll watch Nicky while you try it on."

She shook her head. "I couldn't wear that."

He looked at the sales woman. "What size is it?"

"An eight."

Alik nodded. "It's the right size. Wrap it up and we'll take it along with silver sandals like those on the counter in a size six and a half."

The woman smiled. "Yes, sir."

He handed her his credit card.

Blaire caught him by the sleeve. "Please, Alik." Her eyes implored him. "I know you're angry because I lied to you about a fiancé, but let's not make a farce out of this visit to New York. Let me look around and I'll find me a simple black dress."

What he was about to say was going to hurt her, but it was the only way to guarantee she would agree to wear what he'd bought for her. She'd forced him to fight fire with fire.

"I'm doing this for me, Blaire. So you won't embarrass me in front of my family."

Her gasp told him he'd hit his target dead center.

A few minutes later the clerk returned and draped the garment bag containing the dress and sandals over his arm. After handing him back his credit card, they left in silence for the tuxedo shop he'd seen further down the mall.

Right by the entrance he spied a display of dresswear for children and infants. The smallest tux for a baby turned out to be a one-piece, short-sleeved white suit that snapped between the legs. The bib had been designed to look like the pleated front and collar of a tux with a white satin bow tie fastened at the neck.

Alik started to chuckle. He reached for the outfit and got down on his haunches to show Nicky. "Guess what, little guy? With your white shoes and socks, you're going to be the talk of your grandpa's party."

He placed the tiny tux on the counter, then asked the clerk to show him a black tux of Italian design to enhance Blaire's gown.

"I need a forty-four long with a thirty-four waist, and a sixteen neck shirt."

The clerk held up an outfit for Alik's perusal.

Alik hunkered down by Nicky again. "Do you like it?"

The baby started to move his hands and arms excitedly. Out of the periphery he noticed that for once Blaire wasn't smiling over their son. Her thoughts were on their impending trip to New York. She was terrified about something. He could hardly wait to find out what it was.

Laughing out loud at Nicky's enthusiasm, Alik stood up again. "My son says it will do nicely. Throw in a gray-and-silver striped cravat, a black cummerbund and pearl studs. I'll take a pair of black socks and shoes like those on the floor in a size eleven and a half E."

Once more he laid his credit card on the counter. He purposely let his gaze travel over Blaire who at this point reached down and pulled Nicky from his stroller. Her cheeks were flushed.

It pleased Alik no end that she was so unnerved by the situation, she'd had to resort to using Nicky for a security blanket when he'd been perfectly content in his seat.

"There you are, sir."

Alik thanked the clerk and proceeded to put the shoes and packages into the empty stroller.

Eyeing Blaire he said, "Shall we go?"

With both garment bags over his arm, he pushed the stroller toward the exit. Blaire followed clutching Nicky in her arms.

"When we get back to the hotel, I think it would be wise to have dinner sent to our room. Once the baby is down, we can have an early night. What do you think? Or did you have your heart set on eating out somewhere?"

"My heart isn't set on anything," she answered in a wooden voice.

"If you really don't like the dress I picked out for you, there's still time to return it and find something else."

"The dress is lovely," she admitted at last.

"It will be on you. In fact I dare say the three of us are going to make an entrance that will render my mother speechless. That's a rare phenomenon. One I'm going to enjoy."

When they got into the car, she turned her head in his direction, her expression haunted.

"Alik? I—I know how much you dread going home. How is it you're so eager to fly to New York all of a sudden?"

I can lie as well as you can, my love.

"Correct me if I'm wrong, but weren't you the one who begged me to do this to help smooth Nicky's future?"

"Yes" came her emotional whisper.

"It sounds like you've changed your mind. That's fine with me. I'll head back to Laramie right now. The guys will be thrilled if I show up tonight. We're behind schedule as it is."

Calling her bluff he moved to the other lane. When he saw the exit for Cheyenne coming up, he turned on his right flicker.

"What are you doing?"

"Trying to make you happy."

"No!" she cried in absolute panic.

"No, what?" The more he continued to jab away at her sore spot, the more she reacted like someone with a guilty secret.

"Alik, for heaven's sake! You know we have to go."

"Not if you don't want to."

"I do."

"You're sure."

"Yes."

There was only one person in the car who hated the idea of stepping foot in his parents' home more than he did. That was Blaire. Some force was operating behind the scenes. Alik intended to find out what it was or die in the attempt.

To most people like Blaire, the names Guggenheim, Carnegie, Vanderbilt, Frick, Astor, represented the families of great wealth who in America's past built their fabulous mansions on the North Shore of Long Island called the Gold Coast.

When Alik had said he was flying Blaire to New York to meet his family that first time, she had no idea his home was called Castlemaine Hall, a magnificent Charles II style mansion and gardens built in 1903 on the North Shore as a sixty-acre country estate for his great-great-grandfather John J. Jarman, an important financier and sportsman.

It had been the residence of subsequent Jarmans ever since. Apparently when Alik's father, Robert, had married Estelle Kostas, daughter of the Greek shipping magnate, Spiro Kostas, the Hall became a showplace of eighteenth-century furnishings and fine arts.

At first Blaire had thought Alik was joking when the limousine that picked them up at the airport drove along a tree-lined driveway to a formal courtyard in front of the Hall. She assumed it was one of the famous mansions on the *National Register of Historic* places tourists could visit.

But when two maids of the house staff appeared at the front door to greet Alik like a long-lost son and carry their bags inside for them, Blaire realized this was his home.

She soon learned it was indeed listed on the historic register as an ideal setting for gracious living.

Alik hated it. He called it a criminal monstrosity because it existed at all when so many people were homeless.

The "Blaire Through The Looking Glass," feel never left her during that stay, which should only have lasted two days. But Alik's departure for Kentucky had turned it into one more. And then came the nightmare.

Like déjà vu, the same staff greeted them again, except that this time there were several differences. A half-dozen limousines were parked in the courtyard, and Blaire and Alik had arrived in an ordinary taxi with Nicky in his father's arms.

The maids made such a fuss over the baby, Blaire didn't think they were ever going to move inside the house. It took Alik to notice her fatigue before he asked the staff to fetch their bags.

When they explained that Mrs. Jarman had made arrangements for Blaire to sleep in the blue room as before where a crib had been brought in, Alik countered the plan.

"Blaire and the baby will be staying with me in my bedroom. Will you please have the crib moved there now? Our son needs a nap before tonight's party."

She didn't dare embarrass Alik by protesting in

front of the staff. But she had plenty to say after
they'd climbed the grand staircase and had gained
entrance to his palatial suite in the other wing of the
mansion.

"I can't sleep in here, Alik. I'm not your wife or
your fiancée. By moving me in here with you, the
gossip will spread like wildfire. When your mother
left the trailer last weekend, she was under the impression that I was engaged to someone else. You
might not care if you flaunt convention, but I do."

She didn't like the arrogance of his smile as he
walked around the room with Nicky.

"Our little boy is evidence of the relationship we
shared in the past. Do you honestly believe that separate bedrooms will stop people from construing what
they want? As for Mother, she found us together in
my trailer and will have already put her own construction on things."

Blaire could feel the situation growing out of control. "There's only one bed in here, Alik."

"I'll sleep on the divan as I did as a boy. Nicky?
Did you know I used to lay my sleeping bag on the
top and pretend I was on safari in Kenya or some
such place? I'm sure it's still around here stuffed in
one of the wardrobes. We'll have to take a look."

During the two weeks Blaire had been living with
him, if he hadn't been malleable, she'd at least been
able to reason with him to some degree. But since
he'd taken them shopping in Denver, a change had
washed over him.

Alik had become implacable. It worried her that
she could not longer predict his behavior. In turn,
she'd started getting defensive.

"In a museum ambience like this, I can see why

you created a make-believe world for yourself, Alik, but this is reality and you're grown up now."

"Thank God. *And* old enough to leave this ghastly place for good once Nicky has been presented at court," he mocked bitterly.

"When they bring in the crib, I'll ask for food to be sent up, then we'll nap with Nicky. Neither of us is going to step outside this room until it's time to make our grand entrance in the ballroom tonight.

"Mother wants his presence kept a secret until the crowning moment. To comply with her wishes and not disappoint her, we'll keep our son out of sight."

Alik was so adamant, it frightened Blaire. She turned away from him and began removing their new clothes from the garment bags to hang up before the party. Anything to stay busy while she thought up a plan to get away from him, if only for a few minutes.

Somewhere in this spacious mansion his mother was waiting for Blaire to sign papers drawn up by the family's attorney, which would ensure she could never claim one cent of Jarman money for herself.

But after what had happened last year when Alik had left Blaire alone, he'd obviously decided that this trip he would guard her and the baby to ensure no possibility of repetition.

What terrified Blaire was that his mother would hold her totally responsible if she couldn't figure out a way to escape Alik's attention long enough to carry out the private business agreed upon.

By the time she'd unpacked the new shoes and Nicky's outfit, the maids had brought in the crib. Before they withdrew, Blaire heard Alik ask them to send up a meal.

She didn't think he would fall asleep, even if they

did lie down for a rest before the party. But when he took his shower, there would be a few minutes when she could steal from the room.

But in that assumption she was wrong. After a meal and four hours of relaxation, she disappeared into the ensuite bathroom to bathe Nicky and herself. When they emerged some time later dressed for the party, she discovered a tall, Adonis-like Alik standing in the middle of the ornate room looking resplendent in his tuxedo while he tied his cravat.

She groaned helplessly at the spectacular male image he presented. Only when she'd recovered enough to gather her wits did she realize that while she and the baby had been otherwise occupied, he'd showered in another room, probably the one next door.

That meant there would be no chance to get away from him now. She would have to find some time during the party, and would wait for a signal from his mother.

As soon as Alik saw her, he stopped what he was doing and met her halfway, removing the baby from her arms. His green eyes smoldered as they made a thorough appraisal of her face and body. It took in every detail from the silver sandals on her feet to the profusion of auburn silk flowing to her velvet-clad shoulders.

"W-what do you think of our son?" she asked in a breathless voice.

Slowly his gaze fell on Nicky who was so adorable in his little white suit, Blaire could hardly contain her emotions.

When Alik lifted him in the air and the baby smiled, she glimpsed a liquid sheen bathing his eyes as he looked at his son with a father's love and pride.

She wished she had a camera to catch the sacred moment on film. Barring that, she would always carry a picture of it in her mind and heart.

He finally lowered him to his broad shoulder and turned to Blaire. "It's nine-thirty. Shall we go? It's time."

Grasping her hand in a grip that wouldn't allow her to break away, they left the room and began the long walk down the palatial corridor to the curving staircase.

The sound of music, laughter, people's voices drifted up from the floor below. Blaire dreaded this moment as much as anything in her life, but since Alik was her life, no sacrifice was too great for him.

By keeping her bargain with him and his mother, she would eventually be able to return to San Diego with Nicky. Then the business of visitation and a lifetime of heartache would begin.

The staff must have been told to keep an eye on Alik because his mother was waiting for them in the marble foyer at the bottom of the stairs, looking elegant in a floor-length, deep-red silk gown.

Always her green eyes feasted on Alik with motherly pride. But when she patted Nicky's cheeks and gave him a peck on the forehead, her speaking gaze darted to Blaire with the message that she'd better keep her promise or else.

To carry out her role of gracious hostess to impress Alik, she kissed Blaire's cheek in greeting. "I'll find you," came the warning sotto voice.

"Wait here while I tell the orchestra to stop playing."

When they heard his mother make the announce-ment that Alik had arrived with a special present for his father, Alik's hand tightened on Blaire's.

"No, Alik." She tried to twist out of his grasp. "Go in with Nicky. I'll come in in a minute."

"We're doing this my way or not at all."

He didn't leave her any choice. In the next instant he was half dragging her through the doorway to the accompaniment of cheers and clapping.

Not wanting to make a public display, she stopped fighting him and walked at his side into the eighteenth-century drawing room containing every accoutrement of that time period.

Fifty to sixty guests appeared to be in attendance, not as large a crowd as Blaire had expected. She recognized his brother and sister and their families.

With everyone wearing the most up-to-date fashions, they looked out of place in the surrounding decor. She knew Alik was thinking the same thing as he drew her closer to his parents standing before the enormous hearth.

Mr. Jarman was almost as tall as Alik and probably forty pounds overweight. He wore a similar tux except for the bow tie. A lot of silver was mixed in with the dark blond of his hair.

Though he'd aged some, the older man's light blue eyes were just as aloof and guarded as the last time he'd laid eyes on his son.

Blaire had such a wonderful relationship with her parents, she couldn't relate to the coldness of their greeting. It wounded her all over again to see the two men shake hands when it would have been normal and natural for most fathers and sons to hug and cry after a long absence.

"Father? Happy Birthday. You remember Blaire?"

His parent nodded at her in recognition. "She gave birth to our son on August 19th. May I present Nicholas Regan Jarman. Nicky, this is your grand-father. Give him a smile."

In a gesture that touched Blaire's heart, the baby nestled his dark curly head closer to Alik's neck. While the rest of the room *oohed* and *ahed*, Mr. Jarman lifted him from Alik's arms.

"He looks like you, Estelle." With that comment everyone crowded round to see the baby. "How old is he?" he asked in a voice that sounded curiously gruff.

It appeared that not even someone as seemingly cold and unfeeling as Mr. Jarman could remain totally immune to a child like Nicky.

"Two months," Alik replied with a ring of pride in his voice.

After twenty minutes of constant attention, their normally good-natured baby showed signs that he wanted his bottle and refused to be consoled unless his mommy or daddy were holding him.

Blaire saw this as the perfect moment to take Nicky upstairs. On the way, she could stop off to sign the papers. She caught Mrs. Jarman's eye. The older woman seemed to read Blaire's mind.

"Come on, sweetheart. You're tired. Let's go up to bed." But as she reached for Nicky, Alik surprised her by holding on to the baby.

"Before we say good night," he blurted so that everyone stopped talking, "I have another announce-ment to make."

She couldn't imagine what it was, but Alik's hand still held fast to hers. A sense of foreboding stole through her, causing her to shiver involuntarily.

"Mother? If you'll take Nicky for a moment?"

Mrs. Jarman was totally unprepared to be saddled with her grandson, but Alik hadn't left her with a choice, either.

He looked around the assembled group. "This is indeed a night for celebration. Blaire's gift to me has made me the happiest of men. Now I'd like to thank her in front of my family and friends for all the travail and sacrifice she had to undergo to produce our son.

"Because of a cruel trick of fate, I wasn't aware that she was pregnant with my child until she brought Nicky to me a few weeks ago. Obviously I wasn't present at the delivery.

"No woman should have to live through that experience without the support of the man who loved her enough to get her into that condition in the first place."

No, Alik. No!

"Blaire may have run away from me once, but by some miracle, she came back. Now I'm never letting her out of my sight again."

Before she knew what was happening, she felt him pull her aunt's ring off her finger and slide another one on in its place.

"Tonight I'd like to announce our official engagement. We're going to be married in Laramie, Wyoming, just as soon as we return there. I know you all wish us well in our new life.

"If ever any of you want to visit, you are always welcome. Our trailer will always be open. We'd like Nicky to grow up knowing his grandparents, uncles, aunts and cousins who live in the East.

"One day when the track is forged in a continual line from New York to San Francisco, and the bullet train is fully operational, we'll ride it to visit all of you once more. By that time our little family will probably have expanded.

"Now if you'll excuse us, our son is letting his grandmother know it's past his bedtime. We're leaving first thing in the morning to make the early flight back to Denver. It's been good to see all of you again."

This time when he reached for a tearful Nicky, Blaire was able to pull her hand free of his grasp. While Alik's brother and sister converged on him, Blaire took advantage of the moment to slip out of the drawing room. Mrs. Jarman caught up to her, her eyes flashing anger.

"Did you know about this?" she demanded furiously.

"No! Nothing! I swear it! Alik knows I have no intention of marrying him. I have to stay with him two more weeks, then Nicky and I will be leaving for San Diego."

"I believe you. My son is out of his mind. Come upstairs to my bedroom. Quickly!"

Everything happened in a kind of blur as Blaire followed his mother to their private apartments. As soon as she heard the door close behind her, she saw two men seated at an escritoire with a sheaf of papers.

"Give me the ring."

It was the same diamond Alik had slid on her finger in San Diego a lifetime ago. She pulled it off and dropped it into Mrs. Jarman's outstretched hand.

"Sit down. Mr. Cox will show you where to sign. He's brought Mr. Stanton along to be a witness. I'm going to go back downstairs and detain Alik long enough for you to get back to his room before he does.''

"That won't be necessary, Mother.''

At the sound of Alik's forbidding voice coming from the doorway, Blaire let out a frightened cry.

CHAPTER TEN

A SICKNESS had enveloped her. Slowly she turned around. To her shock, she saw that Mr. Jarman had accompanied Alik to the room. There was no sign of Nicky.

"Mr. Cox? Mr. Stanton? If you wouldn't mind waiting outside, this is a private family matter. But please stay close by in case I need to talk to you."

"Of course." The older attorney cleared his throat. When the two men reached the doorway, Alik pulled the papers out of Mr. Cox's hand. Blaire closed her eyes tightly.

"This is going to take a while," Alik said after shutting the door. "I suggest we all sit down."

Blaire had already found a chair. Her legs would no longer hold her up. His father cupped his mother's elbow and escorted her to a love seat. Alik stood there reading the contents of the papers he'd just taken from the attorney.

When he raised his head, Blaire gasped because the color had drained from his handsome face. In his eyes she saw unspeakable pain.

"According to *this*," he hissed, "Blaire's signature would mean she renounced forever any and all claim to my fortune through her illegitimate son.

"How dare you do this to her, Mother!" Alik's livid voice resounded in the room.

"Don't be angry with her, Alik. It was my idea."

If Blaire didn't defend his mother now, then the worst was going to happen.

"Thank you for saying that, dear." His mother flashed her a smile of gratitude. Blaire knew that for once, it was heartfelt.

Alik looked staggered by the assertion. "*Your* idea?"

She moistened her lips nervously. "Yes. We talked about it in Warwick. You see, I was afraid you might not believe that I was really engaged to someone else. I got worried you would think I'd told you about Nicky solely so that I could get my hands on your money through him over the years.

"Everyone knows you're worth millions in your own right. It would be a natural assumption on your part to assume the worst about me. So I thought that if I could show you legal proof, then you would know beyond a shadow of a doubt that I never expected to capitalize on your generosity."

"It's true, Alik," his mother continued. "Blaire told me she intended to stay with you for the rest of the month to help you with Nicky, then she was going back to San Diego to marry her fiancé."

"*I'm* her fiancé now!" Alik fired back. "She was never engaged to another man. She made him up."

Mrs. Jarman looked incredulous. "Is this true?"

"Yes."

"Then whose ring was that on your finger?"

"My aunt's. But none of it matters, Mrs. Jarman, because despite his determination, Alik and I are not getting married!"

"Alik? Please hand me those papers. I want to sign them, and then find Nicky."

He stared at her as if he'd never seen her before. "Don't you know there's no point in signing them?"

She blinked. "W-what do you mean?"

His head jerked around. "You tell her, Father." The violence in his tone terrified her.

Blaire looked at the older man, but he remained silent.

"*Tell her.* Otherwise, I will."

By now his father had turned as pale as Alik.

"Tell me what?"

"Since he's been struck dumb, I'll ask Mr. Cox to step inside to be witness to what I'm about to reveal."

"No." Alik's father put a hand up, shaking his head. "No, son. This is something I have to do."

Mr. Jarman leaned forward and looked at Blaire. "Young lady? What my boy is trying to tell you is, I disinherited him on his eighteenth birthday."

When the words sank in, Blaire shot out of the chair. "You mean—"

"I mean I had a legal document drawn up, which he signed, renouncing all claim to any money or property for the rest of his mortal life."

Tears gushed down her cheeks imagining Alik's pain. "Why?" she cried from her soul. "What did your son ever do to you to have his birthright taken from him?"

The man's eyes closed for a moment. "He didn't want to be my son anymore."

"You mean he didn't want to follow in your footsteps." She moaned aloud because her sorrow for Alik's unhappiness had gone so deep. "I've heard of people like you. Don't you know what you did?" She almost screamed the words. "He's the finest, the most wonderful, the most superb human being I've ever known in my life.'' Her voice shook.

"He's everything decent and honorable. He's a brilliant scientist and scholar. Alik is a legend at the university where we met. Why do you think out of all the geologists in the U.S., *he* was the one called to cover that vital seminar in Kentucky last year? It's because there's no one else like him!

"Right now he's involved in a project that's going to revolutionize this country's transportation problems for the new millennium. You wanted your youngest child to carry on the Jarman tradition?

"Well he *has*, despite any help or love or support from you! His vision has gone way beyond maintaining the status quo. Instead of living the life of a modern-day Gatsby playing polo or sailing on your yacht, he's chosen the higher path.

"Maybe he doesn't have much money in the bank, but what's in there he got the old-fashioned way. He *earned* it through his own blood, sweat and tears. Of that *I* can bear witness.

"No wonder he didn't want to fly here for your birthday! I'm the one who made him come because I thought it would be better for Nicky to grow up knowing that two diametrically opposed households could put their differences aside for his sake.''

"Enough!" Mrs. Jarman cried in a shaken voice and got to her feet. She kept clutching and unclutching her hands. It was a sight Blaire never expected to see. "Alik—I'm the one who forced Blaire to come. I drove her away the first time by threatening to disown you without a penny if she went through with her marriage to you.

"After your father cut you off, I was afraid we

would lose you altogether if you got married and moved someplace where we would never see you again. I couldn't bear that. You were our shining star.''

Alik was beyond hearing his mother's explanations. His green eyes, naked with pain, searched Blaire's. "Is this true?"

"Yes," she said quietly, then again louder. "Yes." It was heaven to know everything was out in the open. "I—I didn't want you to lose your inheritance because of me.

"When we were dating, you mentioned you came from a wealthy background. But I had no idea what kind of money. There are degrees you know. Castlemaine stands in a class by itself. Once I saw it and realized what you would be giving up for someone ordinary like me, I couldn't do that to you."

"Dear Lord," he whispered. "All this time—all through your pregnancy—you stayed away because of money I never had or wanted."

"Alik, I knew you weren't a person who worshiped money. If you had been that type of man, I would never have fallen in love with you.

"But I know the humanitarian side of you. I thought of all the great things you could do with your inheritance once you had it. All the good. After weighing everything, I decided to break our engagement. I didn't want to hurt you—" She half sobbed. "Forgive me for hurting you, darling."

"Come here to me, Blaire."

She ran toward him.

When she felt his arms close around her, she felt like heaven was near.

"Let's find our son and leave this place," he whispered against her lips.

"Wait!"

They both turned their heads in time to watch his mother approach. Her face was awash with tears.

"This belongs to you, Blaire."

She held out the diamond ring.

Alik picked it up and slid it home. Blaire was dazzled by the love shining from his eyes. "They say the third time's the charm."

Pulling Blaire out the door, Alik started down the hall, intent on reaching the other wing of the mansion where he could be alone with her. There was so much to say to her, he didn't know where to start. And first he just needed to hold her. Love her.

Halfway to their destination, one of the maids met them in the hall. "Your little boy won't settle down no matter what we try."

At the alarm on Blaire's face he said, "It's all right. He's just missing us."

"You also had an urgent call from a Dominic Giraud in Laramie, Wyoming. He said you were to phone him back no matter the hour."

"Thank you for the message."

They both ran the rest of the way to their suite. With every step Nicky's voice grew louder and louder.

"If you'll take care of our son, I'll call Dom."

The euphoria Alik was feeling was so great, he wondered how he was going to contain it.

His eyes never left Blaire who gathered their screaming infant in her arms. Miraculous—a mother's love. The hysterics stopped on cue, as if they'd never been.

He punched in the digits on his cell phone. Excitement made his hands tremble.

"Alik, *mon vieux*?" His friend sounded anxious. "None of us could wait any longer to know what has been happening."

Blinking back tears Alik said, "My vision is crystal clear now. Blaire's wearing my ring again. We're getting married as soon after we get back to Laramie as possible. I'll tell you all about it when we arrive."

"*Dieu merci,*" he proclaimed with a deep sigh of contentment. "My private jet is standing by at the airport there. The pilot has instructions to fly you back to Wyoming tonight. It's my prewedding present to you and Blaire.

"Hannah already talked to our minister, just in case. He says you can be married in three days by special permit. He's willing to perform the ceremony. Zane will stay on in Laramie until the wedding. He plans to stand in as best man with me. We'll phone Blaire's family and tell them to make their flight arrangements. How does a three o'clock ceremony on Wednesday sound?"

For his answer, Alik let out a bark of joy that brought both Nicky's and Blaire's heads around.

"It sounds like I have my answer. *A bientôt*, Alik."

Dozens of candles lit the interior of the tiny Pony Express way station museum, which had been in Hannah's family for generations.

The rustic, log cabin filled with sprays of white roses, gardenias and baby's breath had been transformed into a little church on the prairie.

As Blaire walked through the grass hand in hand with her husband-to-be, she felt as if she had wings on her feet. Wearing the same outfits they'd worn to the party the weekend before, Blaire could believe she was a fairy princess who'd been magically united with her prince.

There'd been an air of unreality as Alik had hustled her and Nicky into a taxi and they'd headed for the airport. The Giraud company jet had just as quickly whisked them away from New York.

Nestled in Alik's arms the entire flight while their baby slept on, they communed in silence, feeding on each other's mouths, laughing, crying, touching, holding.

This precious thing that had happened to them was too wonderful to comprehend. All they could do was show each other how they felt and let their hearts do the talking.

Now they could finally express their feelings with the words they'd been waiting to say for almost a year.

"I, Blaire Regan, take thee, Alik Jarman, for my lawfully wedded husband, to have and to hold from this day forth, both in this world and the next," she added with tears in her voice.

"I promise to love and honor thee, to cherish and adore thee, through the good times and the bad, through sickness and through health, through poverty or wealth."

I know, he mouthed the words and kissed the hand clasped in his.

"I promise to follow thee wherever thou goest, to be thy comfort and thy stay, to be all things thou requires of me. I love thee, my dearest one."

Alik's eyes shone like rare green gems.

The minister cleared his throat.

"Now, Alik, repeat after me. I, Alik Jarman, take thee Blaire Regan to be my lawfully wedded wife."

Blaire listened to every word, absorbing the last of Alik's troth with a sense of wonder.

"I swear to love thee with my dying breath. If I should go before, I swear to wait for thee. If thou shouldst go before me, I swear to live to be with thee, forever and ever. I love thee, beloved."

The minister smiled at both of them.

"For as these two have consecrated their love for each other by exchanging these sacred vows before family and friends, I now pronounce them husband and wife. May their union increase the joy they take in each other in this life. May it continue to be fruitful to sustain them for the world yet to come. Amen.

"Alik, if you have a ring for your bride, you may give it to her now."

Blaire put out her hand for him to add the white-gold wedding band to her engagement ring. She could hardly breathe she was so happy.

The minister turned to Blaire. "Do you have a token of love to give your husband?"

"I do."

Alik's eyes widened in surprise as Blaire's mother stepped forward and handed Blaire the wedding ring she'd bought for him in anticipation of their first wedding date. It had been home in her jewelry box all this time.

In one of Alik's college lectures, he'd talked about opals and had casually mentioned that a bridegroom would be very lucky indeed to be given a black opal doublet, because it was so rare and beautiful.

After Blaire had fallen in love with Alik, she'd gone to a jeweler who bought Australian opals. One day he phoned her and asked her to come in to the shop. There on a cloth of velvet, he showed her a black opal with a layer of green the exact color of Alik's eyes. The stone was expensive, but she had to have it, and saved up for it until she could ask him to set it in gold.

With her heart hammering, she reached for his hand and slid the ring onto his finger.

He stared at it for so long, she wondered if he'd forgotten there was still an important part of the ceremony to go. When he finally lifted his head, he wore the private smile meant only for her, the one that melted her bones and sent her heart quivering. His eyes were like lasers, boring into her soul. They were sending her a message.

I remember giving that lecture. I remember talking about that stone. I love you for remembering. I love you for loving me.

Suddenly his eyes weren't the only part of him communicating. His mouth was doing the most incredible things to hers. As for their bodies, they seemed to be one flesh, one heart. So much love couldn't be contained within these log walls. It needed a place to find expression. But that would have to come later when they would finally be alone.

"Blaire?" Alik touched her bare shoulder gently.

She pretended to be asleep. It was seven in the morning. After a wedding night of pure rapture, she'd been lying awake for an hour, breathlessly waiting for him to pull out of the sleep he'd fallen into around five so they could begin the ritual all over again.

He nudged her once more. "Sweetheart?"

She loved to tease this big, strong, wonderful, intense man of hers. When he rubbed her arm a third time, she made a little moan in her throat.

"What time is it?" she murmured in a woozy voice. "Does Nicky need me?"

His sharp intake of breath was exactly what she wanted to hear. "No. He's with Hannah and Dom, remember?"

"Oh, that's right. Thank heavens. Now we can sleep."

She turned away from him, feigning exhaustion. After five minutes she decided to relent. In truth, her little joke had backfired on her.

"Darling?"

"Yes" came the reply, which bordered on terse.

"I'm sorry. A minute ago you were talking to me. Did you need me for something?"

"No." His voice grated. "It'll keep. Go back to sleep." She felt him turn away from her.

Oh, how she loved him!

"But I'm wide-awake, and what I want won't keep. In fact I've been waiting for you to wake up for over an hour, and if you don't turn around right this minute and make love to me again like you did earlier, you're going to be in big trouble. Do you understand?"

"*Blaire*! You're wicked, do you know that?"

"I know."

"I love you."

"I love you, too."

Another hour later, they lay entwined in each other's arms while they watched the western sky through the trailer window change from streaks of orange to yellow.

She kissed his jaw. "For the first few weeks that you lectured my class, you don't have any idea how many times I used to dream about being with you like this. And I know I wasn't alone. Every girl in there was crazy about you, Dr. Jarman. I still can't believe I'm finally married to you. When I think—''

"Don't!" He covered her mouth and kissed her deeply. When he finally lifted his head he said, "I don't want to think or talk about the past again."

"One day we're going to have to, darling. I saw the look in your parents' eyes when we left their bedroom. They're both suffering."

He swallowed hard. "That's good, because I'll never forgive them for what they did to you."

"Yes, you will, because you're bigger than that. Greater than that."

He crushed her in his arms. "You have a lot more faith in me than I have in myself."

"That's because I'm your wife."

"Yes. You are. In fact I can't remember a time when you didn't feel like my other half. Blaire, I swear the night you ran away from me—''

"I thought we weren't going to talk about the past," she objected, hugging him tighter.

"Dom and Zane always knew something didn't add up."

"They're very intelligent, like you. I love them both."

"They love you. They're the best of the best."

"I agree. Hannah's wonderful, too. Oh, I hope Nicky hasn't kept her up all night."

"Don't worry about it. We'll have plenty of chances to pay them back after their baby's born." There was a pause. "Darling? Are you really all right about living here in Laramie?"

She smiled into his eyes. "Didn't you hear my troth? I promise to follow thee wherever thou goest?"

"We're a long way from the Pacific Ocean."

"I'm exactly where I want to be. You may not realize that yet, but after we've lived together fifty years, you ought to be convinced."

"Convince me now, Mrs. Jarman."

"Love me, Alik," she begged.

"I intend to," he rasped.

He smoothed the hair off her temples and began kissing her face. "I was alone a long time. Despite our problems, despite everything, the last few weeks in this trailer with you and Nicky have brought me the greatest joy I've ever known in my life."

Her breath caught. "I almost died from happiness when you came to the Bluebird Inn to see your son. From that moment on, I would have agreed to anything to stay with you. *Anything.*"

"Let's agree we knew we belonged together. Have I thanked you yet for my beautiful son?"

She smiled. "He is beautiful, isn't he?"

"That's because you're his mother. Lucky man that I am, all this and Nicky, too. What more could a man ask of life? I swear I'll love you forever."

BACHELOR D🎲ds

*An emotional new trilogy by
bestselling author*

Rebecca Winters

Three dedicated bachelors meet thrills and danger
when they each fall captive to an innocent baby—
and clash mightily with three exciting women
who conquer thier restless hearts!

Look out for:

THE BILLIONAIRE AND THE BABY
(HR #3632) in December 2000

HIS VERY OWN BABY
(HR #3635) in January 2001

THE BABY DISCOVERY
(HR #3639) in February 2001

*Available in December, January and February
wherever Harlequin books are sold.*

HARLEQUIN®
Makes any time special.™

Visit us at www.eHarlequin.com

HRBAD

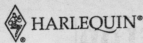

**What happens when you suddenly
discover your happy twosome is about
to turn into a...*family*?
Do you laugh?
Do you cry?
Or...do you get married?**

The answer is all of the above—and plenty more!

Share the laughter and tears with
Harlequin Romance® as these
unsuspecting couples have to be

When parenthood takes you by surprise!

Authors to look out for include:

**Caroline Anderson—DELIVERED: ONE FAMILY
Barbara McMahon—TEMPORARY FATHER
Grace Green—TWINS INCLUDED!
Liz Fielding—THE BACHELOR'S BABY**

Available wherever Harlequin books are sold.

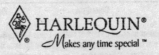

HARLEQUIN®
Makes any time special ™

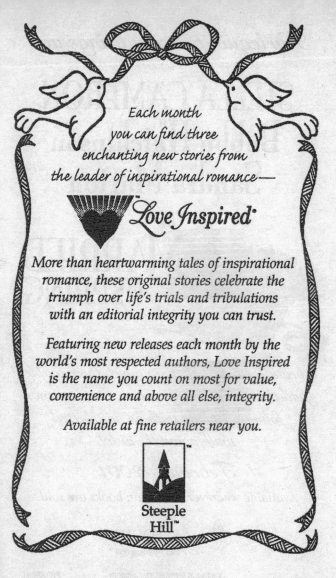